SAPPHIRE AND STEEL
A Star Original

It appeared as the third and last clock stopped its ticking. Steel saw it first, then Rob. Sapphire was also aware of its presence. It was a moving, flickering shape that appeared high up, near the apex of the end wall. It seemed, at first, to be a part of the wall texture itself. As if the plaster of the wall was shifting. Then it appeared to take on a series of quick, broken images. Rob felt that it looked like pieces of old and faded moving-film, except that these images were three-dimensional. Rob also thought that he heard, under the rumbling of the skin-like fabric, the sound of voices that seemed to squeal with laughter or pain, or both.

GW00570749

SAPPHIRE AND STEEL

Peter J. Hammond

A STAR BOOK

published by
the Paperback Division of
W. H. ALLEN & Co. Ltd

A Star Book
Published in 1979
by the Paperback Division of
W. H. Allen & Co. Ltd
A Howard & Wyndham Company
44 Hill Street, London W1X 8LB

Printed in Great Britain by
Hunt Barnard Printing Limited,
Aylesbury, Bucks.

ISBN 0 352 30514 2

Chapter One

Each clock in the house seemed to tick with its own individual sound. In this room alone, the farmhouse-kitchen, there were four clocks, and, through the open doorway, in the downstairs hall, there were two more. One hung on the wall by the cellar door. The other one, its casing made of polished brass, helped to brighten up the dark corner at the foot of the stairs.

At least, Rob imagined that it managed to brighten things. This was an old house, a very dark house, even in daylight.

It was at exactly six-forty-five p.m. that the first clock stopped. It was one of the four in the kitchen and Rob, head down with his homework, did not immediately miss the sound.

When the second clock in the kitchen stopped, at six-forty-five and eight seconds, it might just possibly have registered in Rob's subconscious. Just a slight thinning of sound. But homework on a Friday evening was important to him. Get that done and out of the way, then the whole week-end was his. And he had found that he could always cope with normal, everyday distractions.

Even the sound of his sister's voice, ten minutes earlier, had failed to interrupt his studying. Six year old Helen pleading for one more nursery-rhyme to be read to her at bedtime. And bedtime for Helen was always like part of a ritual. Mum, Dad, a rocking-chair and just one more rhyme, please, before the bedside light was turned off in the top attic bedroom.

The third kitchen clock stopped at exactly six-forty-five and eighteen seconds. This time it did register to Rob, just slightly. Perhaps it was because the faint, familiar voices, from the attic room, stopped at exactly the same moment.

It was still registering in Rob's mind when the fourth clock in the kitchen stopped, three seconds later.

Rob looked up slowly from his work. Only the faint tickings of other clocks in the house could be heard. Apart from those, there were no other indoor sounds. There was the noise of the thin, high wind that persistently blew in from the bay at Deadman's Point and across the flat, open land that surrounded the remote farmhouse. But, inside the house, nothing now, only the quiet sounds from the remaining clocks.

Rob listened for a moment or two. He then put down his pencil, stood up from the refectory table and moved to the open kitchen door.

'Mum?' he called, but there was no answer.

'Dad?'

Nothing.

He had begun to move along the hallway towards the stairs when the clock by the cellar door stopped. By the time he had reached the foot of the staircase, the hands of the brass clock in the dark corner had also twitched to a standstill.

Rob looked up at the flight of stairs. A good antique table on the first landing. Fine prints on the walls. An earthenware jar of dried flowers and pampasgrass that his mother had collected last autumn.

'Helen?' He decided to call her name. After all, it might be one of her jokes, one of her baby-sister tricks. Again, no answer.

Rob had climbed three steps of the first flight of stairs when he heard the other sound. He stopped and listened.

It was the kind of sound that he had not heard before in the house. There was nothing too strange about it at first. It was a murmuring, a vibrant rumbling that grew slowly and steadily louder in volume. Somehow, it was like the highly amplified sound of cloth being shaken. Like the sound of clothes on a washing-line, flapping and straining in a strong wind.

As Rob listened, the sound seemed to reach a kind of peak, like fabric that was being stretched and torn. Like the shrill shriek of ripped muslin. Then silence.

Rob remained standing there, on the third step of the first flight of stairs.

'Dad?' he called yet again. 'What was that noise, Dad?'

The only kind of answer from the top attic room came from Helen. She was making small, hiccupy, sounds. The crying sounds of a frightened child.

Rob began to run up the stairs, two steps at a time. When he reached the third landing, the very top one where the ceilings sloped, he realised that every clock in the house had stopped working.

The door of Helen's attic bedroom was slightly ajar. The warm glow from the bedside lamp highlighted Helen who was sitting on the bed. She wore a nightdress, and her favourite doll, a battered teddy-bear dressed in denim, was on the bed beside her.

To Rob, as he moved carefully towards the door, it should have looked as friendly and as cosy as on any other family evening. But tonight, Helen had her small hands held to the sides of her face. She was moving slightly from side to side as she stared at a fixed point in space. The short, choked, sobbing cries that came from her throat were not unlike the sounds of a small, scared animal.

Rob could also see, beyond the angle of the open door, the flickering of a shadow against the far wall. The shadow of something that shifted quietly and rhythmically, to and fro inside the room.

Rob moved cautiously into the doorway of the room. He stood there for a moment and tried to attract Helen's attention. But his sister would not, or could not, turn her head to look at him.

He counted to five, took a deep breath, then walked into the attic room.

The shifting shadow upon the wall was caused by nothing more than the movement of the rocking-chair which was swinging itself slowly to a standstill.

There was no-one sitting in the chair. In fact, apart from Helen and Rob there was no-one else in the room at all.

Rob looked around him. The large, illustrated book of nursery-rhymes, that his mother always read to Helen, was lying on the floor, as if it had been dropped suddenly.

7

Whenever the book was being read, Rob's father would also be listening and joining in. He would sit upon the very edge of Helen's small dressing-table, as if he had no intention of staying long. Yet he would always be there, his pipe and tobacco pouch set down neatly on the dressing-table beside him, until the child's light was switched off.

The pipe and tobacco pouch were still there now, as if forgotten.

Rob turned his head to look at Helen. 'Where's Mum?' he asked her.

The child said nothing. She lowered her hands slowly from her face and reached out for the teddy-bear.

'And Dad? Where's he?' Rob waited again for a reply, but Helen continued to stare ahead, as if at nothing. She still rocked slowly from side to side, making the small sounds in her throat, as if her real child's tears were trapped inside her.

Rob moved across the room and knelt down to face Helen. He looked at her. But the eyes that looked back, looked past him. They stared out at nothing.

And there was only the silence of the house and the high, pinched sound of the wind outside.

Rob spoke to his sister quietly but urgently. 'Helen,' he said, 'It's me, Rob. Please talk to me.'

A child's eyes in a child's face and an expression that did not belong in those eyes. Then, as if Rob's words had reached her belatedly, she shifted her focus and looked at him.

It was a moment or two before the expression left Helen's eyes and she began to cry. But it was a child's normal tears this time, not the disturbing animal-like whimper that was there before.

Rob put his arms around her. 'It's alright, Helen. It's alright now. I'm here.' And he held her for a while until her crying eased a little.

'So where are they?' he asked once more. 'Where's Mum and Dad?'

Helen looked at him for a moment, as if she had been asked a difficult question. She then appeared to remember.

'Gone.' She whispered quietly.

'Gone? Gone where?'

But Helen was looking at him in the same way again, as if he was asking yet another complicated question.

'Out of the door?' Rob asked her. 'Downstairs?'

Helen shook her head but Rob persisted with his questioning. Some kind of instinct warned him that he had to.

'Well where, then?'

Helen answered with another quiet whisper. 'Just— just went away.'

'Not here in the room? They couldn't have just . . .' And he stopped, because Helen was nodding her head. He knew her that much, knew that she never lied unnecessarily. Neither would she play tricks on him when she knew that he was being serious.

Rob stood up slowly and looked around him at the room. He looked at the book on the floor, the pipe, the pouch, the rocking-chair that had rocked itself still at last.

There were no large cupboards in the room, not even a wardrobe. Helen's clothes were hung in a built-in unit on the landing outside. The door through which Rob had entered was the only door. The room also had only one window. This was fitted with half-length curtains which were drawn to. Rob moved across the room and snatched the curtains open. The small window was shut tight. There was also a child-guard screwed to about two thirds of the window height. Rob tested the guard. It was still fixed firmly in place.

Rob looked out. There was complete darkness outside. Just darkness and the empty sound of the wind. From Rob's window, at the opposite side of the house, one could see a few scattered lights from the houses at Scars Edge, some five miles away on the other side of the bay. But from this window, nothing.

Rob closed the curtains again. He then turned slowly to face his sister.

Still clutching her doll tightly to her, Helen looked back at him, looked at his worried face. 'Just went away,' she said, quietly and earnestly. 'Mama and Daddy, they just went away.'

Rob walked back across the room and knelt down by his sister once more. He looked at her steadily. 'You mean that they disappeared, Helen?' And he watched her eyes carefully as he asked the question. 'Disappeared, here in this room?'

There was no hint of a lie in Helen's eyes. No game. No tricks.

'Yes,' she said, and nodded. 'Just went away.'

Chapter Two

'Oh, I shouldn't think there's anything to worry about, Rob.'.

The voice at the other end of the telephone line sounded familiar but distant. Rob wished it could be closer at hand, that the Unit Beat constable could be right here with him now, making notes in a notebook, taking care of everything.

'They'll be in the house somewhere,' the voice added and Rob pictured the policeman, snug and safe, across the bay, in the small cottage that was nine-parts home and one-part police station.

'But I've searched,' said Rob into the telephone. 'Searched the whole house.'

There was no light in the telephone-box but Rob had managed to balance a hand-torch on top of the empty directory rack.

'Oh, they're bound to be somewhere,' said the voice that was too distant to be of any real reassurance.

The wind was stronger down here near the shoreline. Shot with sea spray, it slashed against the dark windows of the telephone-box. But, inside, the box seemed somehow airtight, stale with the smell of tobacco smoke and salt brine from the summer that had gone.

'Where are you phoning from, Rob?'

The torch began to roll to the edge of the rack. Rob reached for it quickly with his free hand and held on to it tightly. The last thing he needed now was a broken torch and complete darkness.

'The phone box,' he said, 'Down by the summer fishing chalets. Near Deadman's Point.'

'Oh.' And a silence at the other end of the phone. Rob could visualise the policeman, shoes off and feet up by an open fire, considering both his comfort and his duty.

It seemed a long time before the voice spoke again. 'Tell you what, Rob.'

'Yes?' said Rob.

'You get on back to the house and look after your sister, right?'

'Yes, I will.'

'And I'll get Stan to ferry me over,' the voice went on. 'Be there in about an hour.'

'Thank you,' said Rob.

Feeling relieved, almost cheerful, he replaced the telephone receiver.

It was almost a two mile trek back to the house, along a dirt-track approach road, the only approach road. Rob's father had chosen the house because of its isolation. He liked seclusion and preferred to know, as he would put it 'when he was being invaded'. His firm belief was that, between the time it took any visitor to first arrive on the approach road and then reach the house even by car, the inhabitants of the house could have made a cup of tea, a sandwich and settled themselves down by a window to see just who the visitor was. Even at night, the noise of any object on the rough surface of the track road provided enough warning.

With the wind behind him, Rob managed to run back part of the way. He jogged some. Walked the rest. By the time he had reached the obsolete cattle-grid in the road, another of Dad's early-warning system aids, he could see the lights of the farmhouse.

Rob opened the big front door and stepped into the hallway. He closed the door against the wind and the darkness, then locked and bolted it. He switched off the torch, removed his coat, then tried, without success, to make a quick job of smoothing down his wind-blown hair.

He found Helen sitting where he had left her, in the kitchen. She had not moved from the large fireside chair and she still wore, over her nightdress, the blanket that he had wrapped around her before leaving the house. The glass of milk, that he had poured for her, remained untouched beside her.

Rob had somehow hoped that his parents might have returned in his absence with an obvious reason for their disappearance. They might even have made a joke of it at his expense. But Helen's calm, questioning look told him that nothing had changed during his trip to the telephone at Deadman's Point.

'Drink your milk, Helen,' he said, with an attempt at authority. The twelve-year-old taking care of the six-year-old, taking charge of affairs now, in what seemed an otherwise empty house.

He did not feel that convincing, and Helen must have noticed this in her own small way, because she simply stared at him with the same calm but puzzled look on her face.

'Everything's alright,' he assured her. 'So just drink your milk.'

It seemed to work. Although she neither smiled nor looked less troubled, she at least reached forward for her milk and began to sip it.

Rob moved to the kitchen windows, drew back the curtains and looked out at the darkness. 'I've just been to make a telephone call,' he informed her, drawing the curtains to once more. 'I've telephoned the policeman's cottage at Scars Edge.'

Helen nodded over the rim of her glass.

'And I told Constable Daly there . . . You know Constable Daly, don't you?' he asked the small face that was almost hidden by the glass of milk.

Helen nodded yet again. And Rob wandered back to the centre of the room, as if it was the right and proper place to take command from. 'Well, he's coming out here,' Rob announced. 'Constable Daly's coming here. Be here in no time.'

Helen lowered the glass from her face. 'Oh,' she said, a white film of milk helping to form the shape of the word.

Rob moved to her, tugging a crumpled handkerchief from his pocket as he took the glass from her. 'So— so everything's alright, then, isn't it?' he said, wiping her mouth with the handerchief.

Helen gave yet another nod of the head. 'Yes, Rob.'

Rob put his arms about his sister to comfort her, then found that he was holding her very tightly, as if he, too, needed someone, or even something, to reassure him.

The loud knocking at the front door came without any kind of warning. It was sure and precise. Four hard, sharp raps on the knocker, then quietness.

Rob and Helen, both startled, looked up at once. Helen looked at her brother, expecting him to deal with the situation. There was a slight faltering of Rob's voice as he stood up and took command once more. 'Just stay here, Helen,' he said, and walked towards the hallway door.

As Rob entered the hallway from the kitchen, the front door knocker was banged loudly yet again. Four more sharp, precise knocks, identical in sound to the first four.

Rob stayed put for a moment by the kitchen door. He looked along the hallway towards the front door. He estimated that probably a minute had passed between the first bout of knocking and the second. And he imagined that, when a further minute had elapsed, exactly the same sound would happen again. Whoever was out there seemed to make the simple sound of a knock upon a door sound like a mathematical process.

So Rob moved quickly to the door before the next minute was due to expire, but he made no attempt to open the door as yet.

'Who is it?' he said to the locked and bolted door.

'Robert Steven Jardine?' The man's voice, from the other side of the door, seemed as sharp and sure of itself as the punctuated knocking.

'Yes,' answered Rob, surprised at hearing his full name spoken.

The voice outside also sounded cool and flat and emotionless. 'You asked for help.'

'I did. Yes.'

'Then unlock the door.'

Rob's first thought, as he drew back the first heavy bolt, was that Constable Daly had sent one of the Scars Edge villagers on ahead of him. His relief at hearing a voice, any voice, made him overlook the fact that he had heard no-one approach the house.

He drew the second bolt, unlatched the door, then opened it.

The man and woman entered almost immediately. They hardly looked at Rob. Instead, they looked around them at the interior of the hallway as if they were carrying out some kind of inspection.

Rob stared at them. The woman was the most beautiful person that he had ever seen. She had long, fair hair and she was wearing a dress that seemed to shimmer and shift and flow upon her slim figure. She turned to close the door and, to Rob, it seemed as if there was an aura of blueness about her presence, there in the dark hallway. In later years, whenever he remembered her, which was often, his first thought was always the colour blue.

The man had moved to the foot of the first flight of stairs and was looking up at the landing above. He, too, had fair hair. But, as the woman expressed blueness, so the man suggested the colour grey. His smart suit, shirt and tie were somehow neutral. His whole appearance and manner seemed cold, almost metallic.

'I— I don't know you,' said Rob.

The man had finished inspecting the first staircase. He had now moved along the hallway to the cellar door.

The woman was setting the catch on the front door. She then proceeded to slide home the bolts. It was then, as the man opened the cellar door and stared down into the darkness below, that Rob suddenly realised that he had not heard either of them arrive at the house. Neither did they look as if they had been out in a strong wind. Their hair, like their clothes, was immaculate. She could have been at some expensive party, he at some important business meeting.

15

'Only the policeman at Scars Edge...' Rob began to explain.

'The policeman at Scars Edge,' declared the man, without looking at Rob, 'Isn't coming.' He then closed the cellar door and looked past the puzzled Rob, and along the hallway towards the kitchen. 'I've contacted him,' the man said. 'Told him that everything out here is now under control.'

'But it isn't.' Rob protested.

'I know,' agreed the man. 'That's why *we're* here and not him.'

The man then walked down the hallway and into the kitchen. From the moment he had entered the house, the man had not looked at Rob once.

Rob turned to the woman. She smiled at him. To Rob, the smile also radiated blueness. The blueness of a clear, bright sky. But a clear sky on a cool day, not a warm one. And the smile was not the kind of smile that could be ignored. It set the rules. To an older youth, the smile could have seemed like a tease or a joke, or a promise.

'He's a shade too serious,' the woman said, indicating her companion, 'But you'll get used to him.'

'But he's got no right to tell the policeman...' Rob began to complain, but the smile seemed to have complete control over any kind of protest.

'Your parents have disappeared, haven't they?'

'Yes,' said Rob, wondering how the woman knew this.

'And you want them back?'

'Of course I want them back?'

'Safely?'

And the smile had left the woman's face. In its place was a calm but penetrating look that somehow managed to ask the truth and tell the truth at one and the same time.

'Yes,' said Rob, quietly.

'Well, then.' She put out a hand and placed it upon Rob's shoulder. 'Your policeman, with his notebook and his questions, stands no chance in this world of getting them back for you.' Then, before Rob could answer, she added, 'But we do.' And she led him down the hallway towards the kitchen door.

Rob looked up at her as they walked. 'Whatever it is that's happened to them,' he began.

The woman halted by the kitchen door and looked at Rob, waiting for him to finish what he had to say. As if that mattered. As he would always find with her, it was as if she knew exactly what he was going to say next anyway.

'My mother and father,' he said. 'Whatever's happened to them. Is it serious?'

The woman looked at him for a moment or two, with her calm, discerning eyes. 'Yes,' she said, impassively, then led Rob through the open door and into the kitchen.

Chapter Three

'How old would you say the house is?' asked the man. He was standing at the far end of the kitchen, looking through into the small adjoining room that Rob's father used as an office.

The woman was looking around her at the kitchen and its old, farmhouse-parlour furniture. 'At a rough estimate –' she scanned the walls, windows and ceiling '– I'd say two hundred and fifty years.'

The man nodded as he closed the office door then joined the woman in a close scrutiny of the kitchen and its contents.

Helen still sat, wrapped in the blanket, in the big fireside chair. Her head moved from side to side as she watched the man and woman, almost mesmerised by them.

And Rob, too, stood by his sister and watched them. The couple seemed to talk and think and work like two experts.

'Then again, it's very old land, but arable,' said the woman. 'Probably been that way for centuries. There could have been other buildings on the same foundations, back in time.'

'Yes,' the man nodded, then indicated the furniture in the room. 'Genuine antiques?'

'I'd say most of them.' The woman moved to the refectory table. She rested the flat of her long, delicate hands gently upon the surface of the table, as if to test for something. 'This piece alone is about ninety-three and a half years old.'

The man nodded again. 'And the name Jardine?'

'Derived from Old French. The boy's father's name is Henry. His mother's, Sarah.' The woman then pointed to the small, blanket-wrapped figure. 'The child is named Helen.'

Rob stared at the couple in amazement. 'How do *you* know?' he demanded.

18

But the man and woman, still busy with their strange survey, ignored him.

'Old names. An old house.' The man appeared to be addressing the very atmosphere of the room itself. 'Old possessions.' And he paused for a moment as if working out a sum total in his head. 'Lots of— lots of old echoes. Probably too many. Too many echoes.'

'A pressure point, then?' asked the woman.

The man nodded yet again as he continued to take stock of the room. 'Could well be. Could well be it.'

'You seem to know a lot about us.' Rob raised his voice a little this time, determined to get at least a couple of words in.

The woman turned her head slowly to look at him. 'We do. Yes.'

'Then perhaps you'd like to say who *you* are. What your names are.'

The woman considered this for a moment, then switched on the smile that was reminiscent of a clear, cool, blue sky. 'My name is Sapphire.' She made it sound like a proclamation. 'And my friend's name is Steel.'

Rob gazed at her. 'Sapphire?'

'Yes.'

'That's a ...'

'What?'

'Well, that's a— that's a beautiful name.'

'Thank you,' said Sapphire, increasing the smile for Rob's benefit.

Steel broke in on Rob's moment of mild enchantment. 'There seem to be a lot of clocks in this house.'

'Er— yes. My father collects them, makes them work.'

Steel picked up the nearest clock. He looked at it and listened to it. 'So why aren't they working now?'

'Because they all stopped when ...' Rob stopped also, not quite sure how to explain it.

'Yes?' Steel was still looking at him, waiting for an answer.

'Well— they all stopped just before it happened.' Rob waited for Steel to ask him exactly what he meant, exactly what *had* happened. But Steel simply glanced at Sapphire before turning his attention to Rob once more. The man had a way of making each question sound like an ultimatum. 'So where were you when it happened?'

'Me?' said Rob. 'I was down here, right here in the kitchen.'

'And your parents were where?'

Rob pointed up towards the ceiling. 'In Helen's bedroom. At the top. They were reading to her. They read to her every evening before she goes to sleep.'

Steel moved across the room to Helen. He looked down at her for a few moments and Helen's small face looked back up at him.

Helen eventually spoke. 'Mama and Daddy,' she said in her quiet whisper. 'They just went away.'

Steel's face seemed completely unmoved. He turned away from Helen and looked at Sapphire for a moment or two. Rob felt that when the two looked at each other like this, they seemed to isolate themselves from everything and everyone around them.

'I think we'd all better go up to the top room,' said Steel. 'Bring the child.'

Sapphire turned and held out her arms to Helen.

Rob was hoping somehow that Helen would not respond to these strangers. But Sapphire had switched on the smile. Helen shook the blanket from her shoulders and raised her own small arms so that Sapphire could lift and carry her.

Steel was still holding the medium-sized clock. He pointed to a smaller one that was set on the dresser shelf. 'Fetch that, will you?' he ordered Rob.

Rob moved to the dresser and reached up for the small clock.

The procession climbed the first flight of stairs. Steel, carrying the medium sized clock, kept his eyes fixed firmly on the stairs and the shadows above. Rob was close behind him with the second clock. Sapphire, cradling Helen in her arms, followed them, the teddy-bear doll swinging from the child's hand.

They reached the first landing, crossed it, then began to

climb the second, narrower flight of stairs. No-one spoke on the way up.

The second landing was smaller than the first. A vase and a short-case clock were its only ornaments. The clock had stopped at just after a quarter to seven. A cupboard-stair door, that led to the third flight of stairs and the attic room, was still open as Rob had left it.

The small procession reached the second landing. Steel halted there. He looked around him, taking note of the case clock as he did so. Sapphire, Rob and Helen watched him and waited.

'What did you hear?' asked Steel.

The question came unexpectedly, catching Rob withought a thought in his head.

'Sorry?'

Steel looked at Rob with an expression of weary impatience, as if he, Steel, had every right to ask questions without warning and was also entitled to immediate answers. 'What did you hear when the clocks stopped?'

Rob thought about it. 'Well, there was a kind of silence.'

Steel regarded him with the same expression on his face. 'I want to know what you heard, not what you didn't hear.'

Rob apologised yet again. 'Oh, sorry.' Then he remembered. 'I heard Helen crying.'

Steel wandered towards the open stair door and peered up at the landing above. The warm light from Helen's bedroom lamp reflected on the sloped ceiling of the tiny landing. Just a small glow that helped to accentuate the shadows.

'And that was all you heard?' Steel was still looking up through the cupboard-stair door.

'Well, no. There was this sound.'

Steel turned his head slowly to look at Rob. 'What kind of sound?'

Rob found it hard to explain.

'Describe it.' Steel insisted.

Rob tried his best. 'It was like a—well, it was like a rumbling sound at first,' he said, causing Steel to glance at Sapphire. 'Then it became different. It became a kind of tearing sound.'

But Steel was already leading the way through the

cupboard-stair door and up the steep steps to the attic.

When the four of them had reached the small, angled landing, Steel raised his hand. The party halted there.

The door to the attic bedroom was still ajar. The light, from the small lamp inside the room, highlighted their faces.

Steel nodded at Sapphire. It was like a kind of signal. Sapphire set Helen down, then moved to the open doorway and stood there.

Rob watched her. Sapphire had her hands raised, palms facing outwards. She seemed able to examine and measure an atmosphere with the same skill that she used to analyse a solid object.

'Yes,' she said and lowered her hands. 'It's here. Somewhere.'

Steel leaned forward and took the handle of the attic bedroom door. 'In this room?'

Sapphire nodded. 'It could well be in that room, yes.'

Steel pushed the handle and the door swung inwards so that, from the landing, the whole of the inside of the room could be seen. The room was just as Rob and Helen had left it. The crumpled bedclothes, the fallen book, the rocking chair, the pipe and the pouch.

'So where have they gone?' asked Rob.

Steel and Sapphire stared into the room without answering him.

'My mother and father,' Rob tried again. 'Where have they gone, please?'

Steel and Sapphire turned slowly to look at Rob.

'I'm afraid we can't afford to tell you that right now,' said Steel.

'Why not?'

Once again, Steel did not answer. He turned back to the doorway of the room.

'Look, I want to know.' Rob raised his voice a fraction. Sapphire was regarding him with the calm, cool look, but Rob decided to make a bit of a stand at last. 'I've every right to know. I live here, remember?' he said, maintaining his stand.

'Yes,' Sapphire was still looking at him. 'You live here.'

'And Helen. Helen lives here as well.' Rob moved towards his sister. He took her hand and eased her away as far as he could in the cramped space of the attic landing, just far enough to separate himself and Helen from the two adults.

Steel had turned to watch him.

'I mean, you two— you arrived here— just like that.' Rob tried to click his fingers but it did not work very well. 'This place, well, you can hear cars or people approaching this place from miles away. But you two— you arrived— just like that.' He decided not to attempt the finger click a second time.

'One-point-nine-four miles to be exact,' said Sapphire.

Rob stared at her, taken out of his stride. 'What?'

'The distance of approach to this house.'

'Oh,' said Rob, deciding to work that one out later. 'Anyway, I want to know. Now.' And he stood there defiantly, holding his sister close to him. Helen simply looked from one person to the next, as if she were waiting patiently for an adult argument to go away.

Sapphire continued to look at Rob for a moment or two, then she smiled. 'Alright then,' she conceded.

Steel interrupted her quickly. 'It can't be explained to him.'

'It can, in a way,' said Sapphire. 'But not by you perhaps.'

Steel jabbed a finger at the attic bedroom. 'If we are going to re-construct what happened in there . . .'

'Then maybe he *should* know things.'

Steel looked at her then decided to say nothing as Sapphire moved towards Helen and took the child's hand in hers.

'There is, if you like, a corridor,' said Sapphire to Rob.

Rob stared at her.

'And the corridor— again, if you like— is Time. It surrounds all things. It passes through all things.'

Rob continued to stare at her. 'Time?' he asked.

Sapphire nodded. 'Time.' She put her arm about Helen's shoulders and drew the child close to her as she continued to address Rob. 'You can't see it. Only now and again. Perhaps a glimpse, that's all. But even that is dangerous. Also, you cannot enter into Time.' The smile left her face. In its place was the calm, cool look. It was a look that somehow helped to illustrate her theme. The look itself seemed ageless, as if the blueness, that she radiated, was somehow both the colour and the secret of time.

Rob stared at her as she continued with her explanation. 'But, once in a while, Time can try to enter into the Present. Break in. Break through. Take things. Take people.'

Rob began to realise. He glanced towards the attic bedroom, then back.

'But this— this corridor— it's strong, you see.' Sapphire was still looking at Rob as she spoke. 'It has to be. But sometimes, in certain places, it becomes weakened. Like fabric. Worn fabric. And when there is pressure upon that fabric . . .'

Rob recalled the sound he had heard. 'Time comes in?' he asked.

Sapphire nodded. 'Time comes in. Reaches in. Takes what it wants.'

Rob looked at the room once more, then at Steel, then back to Sapphire. He looked stunned.

'And we think that Time has broken through in that room,' said Sapphire. 'Broken through the fabric – and taken your parents.'

Rob was still staring, open-mouthed, as Steel moved towards the attic bedroom door.

'Come on,' he ordered, as he walked into the room.

Chapter Four

Steel had wound up the two clocks from the kitchen. Rob and Helen had watched him as Sapphire performed her customary task of sensing and testing the atmosphere of the room. Now Steel was winding a small clock with a cartoon face, that had stood on the narrow bookshelf in the attic bedroom.

The noise of the wind outside sounded thin and solitary as usual, up here at the top of the house. But, to Rob, the ticking of the three clocks inside seemed to compensate. He felt like telling Steel that it sounded like 'old times' to hear them working again. But Steel did not seem to be the kind of person who would appreciate a joke, so Rob said nothing as Steel began placing the three clocks at carefully strategic positions within the room.

'So what happened to the clocks?' Rob asked.

Steel was arranging the larger of the two kitchen clocks so that he could see its face from any angle in the room. 'They wound themselves down,' was his only answer.

Rob stared at the nearest clock. 'But my father winds those every day.'

'I expect he does,' said Steel, standing back to survey his arrangement.

'So how can clocks wind themselves down in just a fraction of a second?'

There was no answer from Steel, so Rob turned to look at Sapphire. 'It isn't possible,' he said to her.

'I know,' she gave him just a trace of the smile. 'And yet it's happened.'

Rob turned to look at the clocks again but found that Steel was looking at him.

'You say that you were in this room with your parents and your sister before going downstairs?'

'That's right,' Rob answered.

'And that's the last you saw of your parents?'

'Yes.'

'So where was the child?'

Rob indicated. 'Sitting up in bed.'

Steel nodded to Sapphire, who led Helen to the bed, lifted her and sat her upon it.

Steel looked at Rob. 'Like that?'

'More or less, yes,' said Rob. He then saw that Helen was looking at him. She seemed troubled and unsure of things. 'Just stay there, Helen,' he said to her gently. 'Just do as they say and stay there. Everything's alright.'

'Yes, Rob,' whispered Helen, managing a small, nervous smile.

Steel continued to organise Rob and the room. 'And your father was where?'

Rob pointed towards the small dressingtable. 'He always sat on the edge of there.'

'Sit there, will you?' ordered Steel.

Rob stared at the man. 'What?'

'I said, sit there. Just sit as he was sitting when you last saw him.'

Rob thought about it for a couple of seconds. He then walked to the dressingtable and sat down on the very edge of it. He looked down at his father's pouch and pipe that were now beside him. He reached down for them.

'And please don't touch anything.'

As Rob withdrew his hand he wondered why Steel ever bothered to use the word 'please'.

'And your mother was sitting in this chair?' Steel was pointing at the rocking-chair.

'Yes.'

Steel nodded yet again to Sapphire. She walked to the rocking-chair and sat in it. Steel then reached down for the book of traditional nursery-rhymes. He showed the book to Rob. 'And this was the book that your mother was reading from?'

'Yes.'

'Aloud?'

'Yes.'

As Steel handed the book to Sapphire, Rob remembered how his mother would read from the book, with his father sitting watching, and he realised fully at that moment just how much he missed them and the warm, safe comfort that they always seemed to provide. He also realised that he had taken that comfort too much for granted. He never once wanted to stay around while nursery-rhymes were being read. He had felt that he was slightly above all that. Now he wished that he had stayed. Just once. Just on that last occasion. Perhaps he could have helped, could have done something when this Time thing, whatever it was, came into the room.

Steel's voice interrupted his thoughts. 'Which particular rhyme?' Then, before Rob could adjust from those thoughts, 'Which particular rhyme was being read aloud when the clocks stopped, when you heard the noise?'

'I wasn't here, was I? I was downstairs,' said Rob.

Questions, coming from Steel, were like part of an interrogation. 'It is important to know the exact rhyme.'

'Well, I'm sorry but I don't know it.' Rob protested. As always, Sapphire spoke at just the right moment, easing the tension. 'Helen,' she said to the child. 'Do you remember which nursery rhyme it was?'

Helen said nothing.

'She's not very talkative at first.' Rob said, glad to break off the exchange with Steel. 'Not very talkative with strangers.'

Sapphire gave Rob the cool, bright smile which immediately made him want to assist her at any price. 'Then you try,' she suggested.

Rob looked across the room to his sister. 'Helen,' he called. She looked at him. 'When Mama—' Rob decided to choose his words carefully, 'Just before Mama went away. Do you remember?'

Helen gave only the slightest of nods.

'What was she reading to you? Which nursery-rhyme?'

'Don't know,' said Helen, quietly.

'You do know, Helen. You must know.'

Helen shook her head but Rob persevered, trying to be as gentle and as persuasive as possible. 'So which one? Tell us, Helen, please.'

Helen sat there on the bed for a long moment. She moved her eyes, but not her head, to look first at Sapphire, then at Steel, then back to Rob.

'Best one.' Helen whispered.

'Your favourite?' Rob felt pleased with his progress ' "Ring-a-ring o' roses"?'

Helen nodded once more and gave a slight, almost shy, smile.

Sapphire was already turning the pages of the book. ' "Ring-a-ring o' roses" is derived from the times of the plague,' she told Steel. 'Could be one more factor. Even the final one.' She found the page in the book.

Steel had moved to the centre of the room. He looked at the three clocks in turn, then proceeded to study the walls and ceiling of the attic room. Rob and Helen watched him.

'Read the rhyme slowly.' Steel instructed, as he kept a watch on the room. 'Stop whenever I raise my hand. When I lower my hand, continue.'

'Right,' said Sapphire, the open book ready on her lap.

'But, if I shout to you to stop, then stop immediately.' Steel was still watching the walls and ceiling. 'If I say, "Back, back", reverse the order of the words.'

'I know.' Sapphire nodded and Rob noticed that her face was very serious now. The almost lazy coolness had gone. In its place was an expression of deep concentration.

'But carefully.' Steel warned her, looking equally serious. 'Not one mistake. Not even one letter said wrongly.'

Sapphire nodded and waited, the book now raised in her hands. Rob was watching. Helen watched also, the teddy-bear doll still held close to her. The varied, but steady ticking of the three clocks.

'Begin now,' said Steel as he watched the room.

Sapphire began to read slowly from the book, pausing for long moments between each set of words. *Ring-a-ring o' roses. A pocket full of posies . . .*'

Helen smiled as she heard the words of her favourite rhyme. Then Steel raised his hand, just slightly, and Sapphire stopped reading. Steel looked carefully at the walls and the ceiling, from his position in the centre of the room. He then lowered his hand.

'*A-tishoo! A-tishoo!*' read Sapphire from the book. 'We all fall down.' She waited a moment but there was no further signal from Steel. '*The king has sent his daughter . . .*'

Then something. A very faint rustling sound somewhere in the room. Steel raised his hand quickly and Sapphire immediately stopped reading. Steel looked around at the room. Nothing could be seen although the faint rustling sound continued.

Then the larger of the kitchen clocks stopped. Steel glanced quickly at the clock. Then, watching the room once more and with the steady concentration of a man defusing a time-bomb, he lowered his hand.

'*To fetch a pail of water . . .*' read Sapphire, from the book.

The sound increased. It was like a shaking, a pattering, a fluttering.

'*A-tishoo! A-tishoo!*' read Sapphire.

The sound deepened now in intensity and became more of a vibrant rumbling, more like the sound that Rob had heard earlier that evening.

'*We all fall down.*'

Rob could imagine giant sails in a wind. There was even a slight current of air in the room now, like a light breeze that picked at Steel's hair. And Rob could almost visualise the fabric as it shook and strained under pressure. He imagined a fabric like skin. A living fabric. And he began to feel frightened. Even Sapphire had glanced up from the book. But Steel's hand remained lowered as he focused his attention on the room, looking for the very source of the sound.

The cartoon hands, on the face of the bedroom clock, stopped. Only the one small clock remained working.

'*The bird upon the steeple . . .*' read Sapphire.

It appeared as the third and last clock stopped its ticking.

Steel saw it first, then Rob. Sapphire was also aware of its presence. It was a moving, flickering shape that appeared high up, near the apex of the end wall. It seemed, at first, to be a part of the wall texture itself. As if the plaster of the wall was shifting. Then it appeared to take on a series of quick, broken images. Rob felt that it looked like pieces of old and faded moving-film, except that these images were three-dimensional. Rob also thought that he heard, under the rumbling of the skin-like fabric, the sound of voices that seemed to squeal with laughter or pain, or both.

Steel raised his hand and Sapphire stopped reading at once. The movement on the patch of wall, and the half-seen pictures, seemed to freeze. The sound stayed at a constant level.

Steel took a few cautious steps towards the end of the room and halted. He looked up at the patch of wall.

Rob turned anxiously towards Sapphire, but Sapphire had anticipated his concern. She looked at him and put her finger to her lips.

Steel began to lower his hand very slowly and Sapphire spoke the next line of the rhyme simultaneously.

'Sits high . . .'

The shapes on the wall began to move. The sound began to increase.

'Above . . .' continued Sapphire, her eyes moving from the book, to Steel, to the wall, to the book again. And Rob and Helen stared, wide-eyed, at the section of wall as the voice sounds and the fabric sound seemed to overlap, and the shifting pictures and shapes jostled and mingled into one another.

' . . . the people.' Then, as Sapphire raised her voice so that the last two words of the rhyme could be heard, the patch of wall began to move outwards, as if something behind it was pushing at it. As if the wall itself was melting.

Steel shouted loudly. 'Stop!'

Sapphire stopped reading.

'Back! Back!' shouted Steel. 'Take it back!'

'People, the, above,' read Sapphire slowly. 'High, sits.'

Rob stared as the wall appeared to check its melting effect.

'*Steeple, the, upon, bird, the.*' As Sapphire continued to read the words backwards, the pictures upon the wall began to fade. So, too, did the sounds. By the time Sapphire had read the words '*Down, fall, all, we,*' the patch of wall had returned to normal and the sounds had completely died away.

'Down fall all we?' said Steel, in the now quiet room, and it was like a question put to the room itself. And Rob watched Steel as the man breathed out deeply and slackened his body, like someone who had just performed a strenuous mental task.

It was Helen who broke the moment of relaxed stillness. 'Pictures,' she said, pointing a small finger at the far wall. 'Saw pictures.'

'Yes, Helen. But it's alright now,' said Rob. And he moved across the room to the bed and sat down next to his sister.

Sapphire had closed the book. She was looking at Steel as if waiting for his next move.

'The fabric you were talking about,' Rob began, trying to catch Sapphire's eye. 'Was it . . .?'

But Sapphire was still looking at Steel, as if there were more important questions than Rob's to be asked at that particular moment. 'We can't seal it yet, then?' she asked Steel.

Steel looked up at last. 'No,' he said. 'Not until we've brought those people back.' And his moment of relaxation was over. Once more, he was businesslike and coldly efficient. 'I want that book taken downstairs and destroyed.'

Sapphire nodded as she rose from the chair, the book tucked firmly under one arm.

'Has the child somewhere else to sleep?' Steel was switching off the bedside lamp.

'Yes,' said Rob. 'There's a spare bed in the room next to mine.'

'Where?'

'Next floor down.'

'Then take her there.' Steel picked up the two kitchen clocks, moved to the door and held it open, ushering the others out from the room that was now dark and empty looking.

'And is there a key to this door?' asked Steel, as they moved out on to the landing.

31

Rob shook his head. 'No. It was lost years ago.'

Steel pulled the door to, slamming it tightly shut. 'Then I want no-one to enter this room. Is that understood?'

'Yes,' said Rob.

'Not until we've done what we have to do.'

Rob nodded automatically, wondering what it was that had to be done, but Steel was already descending the stairs. Sapphire, holding Helen's hand, followed him down.

Rob was still looking at the closed door of the room as Steel switched off the top landing light from below.

Rob turned quickly and hurried down the stairs after the others.

Chapter Five

Sapphire had put some kind of a snack meal together for the two children. Helen was then put to bed. When Rob peeped into the spare room, an hour or so later, long after the clocks had all been rewound once more, he found his sister fast asleep.

Sapphire was alone in the kitchen when Rob returned. The hob-lid of the stove was open and Sapphire was burning the nursery-rhyme book, dropping the pages, a few at a time, into the flames.

It was as Rob closed the kitchen door behind him and was about to tell Sapphire that Helen was sound asleep, that he realised. He stopped and stared across the room.

When Sapphire and Steel had arrived at the house earlier that evening, they carried not one bag or suitcase between them. Yet now, Sapphire was standing by the stove and she was dressed in a completely different outfit. Rob looked hard at her. Even her hair-style had changed. She looked, to Rob, like a woman he had once seen in an old nineteenth century picture.

Sapphire looked around at him, noticed his stare, then realised.

'Oh.' She gave him the smile. 'I suppose I've surprised you.'

'Well . . .' Rob began, still puzzled.

'Only I fancied a change,' said Sapphire, turning back to the stove. 'Steel complains now and again,' she added as she dropped more pages into the open hob of the stove.

Rob moved slowly across the room, still staring at her.

'He says I shouldn't use Time as if it's— well, as if it's some kind of wardrobe.' She broke the back cover of the book and dropped the pieces into the fire. 'But he's so serious and I get bored wearing the same . . .'

'But where did you get them?' Rob was still staring at her.

'What?' asked Sapphire innocently as she poked pieces of book down into the stove.

'The clothes.'

'Oh,' she smiled. 'They're not real. These ones aren't real.'

'Not real?'

'No.' Sapphire set the poker down and dropped the last few pieces of book into the open hob. 'Look.'

Rob looked.

'These were a favourite of mine last week.'

Rob was still looking at Sapphire as her outfit changed yet again. This time it was a nineteen-forties style. Clothes, shoes, hair, make-up, everything.

And Rob, although he could not understand, accepted it totally and without question. Whoever she was, whatever she was, he knew, deep inside himself somewhere, that he accepted Sapphire. He also knew, then, that this complete acceptance that could not be accounted for, would be with him for the rest of his life. Perhaps he could not trust her. He was not sure of this now but somehow it did not seem to matter. Whatever the cost to come, he accepted her and believed in her at that moment in time. And, as his mind and his soul and his body told him this, he found that he was looking into her eyes and beyond them. It was only a glimpse. A hint. It was as if those eyes were clear blue shutters that were capable of opening and showing him times and worlds that he had never seen and never would see.

'So what do you think, Rob?'

She turned, to show him the complete effect of the outfit and the moment passed.

'I think it's—' Rob tried to put the right words together. 'I just think that . . .'

'What?' asked Sapphire.

'That— well, I just think that you're beautiful.'

'Thank you,' said Sapphire. She put the hob-lid back on the

stove and the glow from the fire was shut in. So, too, were the images that Rob had seen in her face.

'The corridor thing, have you ever seen it?' asked Rob, trying to keep the fascination going.

'Not properly.' Sapphire replied as she placed the poker back at the side of the stove. 'It's both difficult and dangerous to see. Time always is. You can't go backwards into Time to look. Or forwards.'

'Then how can you see it?'

'You see it when it breaks in, of course.' And she seemed a little tired of the explanation as she moved to the sink to wash her hands.

Rob moved to help her. He turned on the tap and handed her some soap and a towel.

'We had this assignment once,' said Sapphire.

'Assignment . . .'

Sapphire nodded as she washed her long, sensitive-looking hands. 'On a ship, of all things.'

'A ship?' Rob pursued it, intrigued.

'Yes. Time breaking through in the middle of the ocean, would you believe?' She took the towel from Rob. 'Thank you.'

'And is this . . .?' Rob began.

Sapphire looked at him.

'Is this— well, you being here. Is this also an assignment?'

Before she could answer him, Steel had appeared in the doorway of the kitchen. He watched them.

'Sorry,' said Sapphire to Steel. And, during the fraction of a second that it took to return the towel to Rob, she was back in her original clothes.

Steel walked slowly into the room. 'Perhaps, when you've finished telling the boy all about the nicer aspects of our job,' there was an edge to Steel's voice. 'You'll also tell him about the dangers.'

'He knows about them.' Sapphire replied.

'Enough about them? Enough about the dangers in this house?'

Sapphire said nothing as Steel walked slowly to Rob and

35

stared at him for a moment or so. 'This corridor, it's immense,' said Steel. 'So don't try to imagine it.'

'No,' said Rob.

'Because Time is immense.' Steel held up finger and thumb, indicating a measure. 'So try to imagine instead, if you're capable of it, Mankind, or the existence of mankind, as approximately one inch in length.'

Rob nodded as Steel placed his finger and thumb approximately one inch away from the boy's face. 'Then compare it with this corridor called Time, which is, say, a thousand million miles long.'

Rob tried to focus on the finger and thumb that were held close to his face.

'Mankind— one inch.' Steel continued. 'Time and the unknown— a thousand million miles. Just compare them. Got it?'

'Yes, I think so,' lied Rob.

'Good.' Steel removed his hand. 'Because I think you've already witnessed a fraction of those dangers this evening, whether you recognised them as dangers or not.' Steel pointed. 'Upstairs.'

'Oh, I realise . . .' Rob began to say.

'Because some things have access to that so-called corridor.' Steel began to cross the room as if he had finished what he had to say. He began to check the clocks.

'Things?' Rob asked nervously.

Steel turned to look at Rob once more. 'Yes. Things.'

'What kind of things?' asked Rob.

Steel glanced at Sapphire, as if to say, 'Just what have you started?' He then looked back at Rob.

'Things,' he said the word again, making it sound even more sinister. 'Things from the very beginnings of Time. Or things from the very end of Time. Take your pick.'

Rob looked at Sapphire, then back to Steel.

'And these things are— these things are in that corridor?' Rob half-whispered the question.

Steel nodded. 'Forever moving along it. Backwards and forwards.'

The fear inside Rob was sudden and sharp, like a pain. It was a fear for his parents that was not helped by the jumbled thoughts in his head. And he found that his mind seemed to be confused by the bright magic of Sapphire and the cold logic of Steel.

He could hear the man's words through the mild chaos of his thoughts and feelings. 'And they move to and fro in that corridor.' Steel's voice continued with its warning, with its threat. 'Ever looking. Ever searching. Always trying to find a way in, trying to find a way through the fabric.'

Helen could not sleep properly. The events of the evening and being put to bed in a strange room probably caused the unrest. And so she awoke, reached for her teddy-bear doll, then climbed out of bed.

She opened the door of the spare bedroom then, dressed only in her nightgown, she moved out on to the landing.

She thought, at first, that she might go downstairs. She could hear Rob, Steel and Sapphire talking in the kitchen below. But, in her young mind, there was time to see them later. Time enough to talk to them afterwards.

Helen moved to the cupboard-stair door and opened it. She peered up towards the dark attic landing.

'Look for Mama and Daddy, shall we, 'Becca?' she asked the doll.

She rocked the doll in her arms, then looked up at the landing once more. 'See the pretty pictures again, shall we?' And she made the teddy-bear doll nod its head in answer.

Still cradling the doll, Helen began to climb the steep, dark stairs to the attic above.

'But what made them come in?' Rob was still trying to get things straight, still trying to understand it all in his mind. 'What made the things choose this house?' he asked. 'Why our home?'

'We've already explained that to you,' said Steel. 'The fabric is here. The echoes of the past, all the right— or wrong—ingredients are here in this house. Therefore the pressure-point was here.'

'Upstairs in Helen's room?' said Rob.

Steel nodded. 'But we've stopped them. We've held them. We've destroyed the final echo. The last ingredient. The trigger.'

'The trigger?' whispered Rob.

'Yes,' said Sapphire, and pointed to the stove. 'You watched me burn it, didn't you?'

'I watched you burn the book, yes. Was that the trigger?'

'Not quite,' said Sapphire. 'But one particular line was. The next line. The line that Steel prevented me from saying. Remember?'

And Rob remembered the rhyme read aloud and the wall that pushed outwards and the terrible sound. 'Yes, of course I remember.'

'Well, that was the trigger.' Sapphire was looking at Rob steadily. 'One particular line, from one particular nursery rhyme, said aloud in one particular room. Helen's room.'

Helen had opened the door of her bedroom and she had switched on the bedside lamp. She now knelt upon the bed, the teddy-bear doll cradled upon her knees. She did not miss the book because she had a good memory for her age and therefore knew her favourite nursery-rhyme by heart. Every last word and letter of it.

Helen began to swing the doll to and fro as she chanted the rhyme. *'Ring-a-ring o' roses. A pocket full of posies . . .'*

In the kitchen, the wall clock stopped first. Steel had already hurried across the room. He dragged open the hallway door as the second clock stopped.

The hallway clocks also ceased their ticking, first one, then the other as Steel ran to the foot of the first flight of stairs.

Steel was looking up at the landing above, listening for

something, as Sapphire and Rob hurried along the hallway to join him.

They could just hear, from the very top of the house, the faint sound of Helen's voice as she recited the rhyme.

'The king has sent his daughter . . .' As the child's chanting voice floated down to them from the attic room Steel, Sapphire and Rob were already running up the first flight of stairs.

By the time they had reached the first landing, Helen's voice could be heard more clearly. *'To fetch a . . .'* The child seemed to have forgotten the sequence.

Steel, Sapphire and Rob had crossed the landing and were climbing the second flight of stairs as Helen remembered. *'. . . To fetch a pail of water. A-tishoo! A-tishoo . . .!'*

They heard the rushing, rumbling sound as they reached the second floor landing. And, as they clambered quickly up the steep attic stairs, the sound had already increased and was growing even louder.

'The bird upon the steeple.'

· 'Helen!' Rob found himself shouting as Steel shoved open the door of the attic room.

'Sits high above the people.'

And Helen was there in the room, cradling the doll, her face reflecting the light that was already spilling from the wall. The light breeze blew through the room and the jumbled, restless shapes were there, like a part of the radiant light. But the shapes moved faster now, so that the wall was beginning to lose its natural form. To Rob, it no longer resembled a wall. It was like a lot of different places somewhere else. A lot of voices. A lot of people. A madness. A confusion. It was, to him, like the worst of the cold, feverish dreams that you woke screaming from during an illness. The most disturbing nightmare snatched from sickness and thrust forward and magnified a thousand times.

As the sound grew to a high pulsating screech that seemed to cut through the ears and the skull and the nerves, Rob found that he could not look away from this tumbling mass of light and noise. It appeared to be advancing into the room, advancing towards him, gaining ground and space as it spread itself, so that the room appeared to be proportionately smaller. It was as if the attic bedroom was being absorbed, as if the shifting, growing light was soaking up all that was real and sane and safe. And, above it all, was the terrible tearing sound.

'Hold her! Hold the child! Steel's voice seemed as faint as a voice in a storm. 'It's too late to say the rhyme back. Just hold the child!'

Then, among the shapes and half-seen figures that moved within the area of light, Rob saw the shadow of his mother. He recognised her by the slow, easy way she walked. Like someone who was never in any hurry. She was moving towards him. She then disappeared and reappeared again further back among the shapes, moving forward once more but smaller in perspective, as if the mass of light had a depth of its own. Then she was gone again. To Rob it was like watching a distant swimmer on a hot day, when sky and sea and haze merge with equal brightness. He thought, too, that he heard her voice under the shrill sound. On impulse, he pressed his hands hard against his ears and stumbled towards the area of light.

He felt himself grabbed and dragged backwards suddenly and violently.

Steel jerked Rob towards the open doorway, then released him. Rob felt a gentler hand take him by the shoulder. It was Sapphire. She was standing outside the door and holding Helen close to her.

The area of light, the moving, shifting mass that was once a wall, now filled the room and was spreading towards them and the open door, throwing out its reflecting light as it moved.

Steel reached out again. This time he snatched the doll from Helen's hands. Before she could cry out in protest, Steel had leaned forward and tossed the doll into the centre of the light source.

The teddy-bear doll did not complete its journey through the air. It did not fall to the floor. Rob saw it reach the area of light. There was a grabbing, snatching sound and the doll disappeared. It seemed to be sucked into the mass of light.

Steel pulled the door to and slammed it shut for the second time that evening. From inside the room, the sound died, like

40

something that had been switched off. But the glow flickered around the edges of the door for a few moments. Then that also died.

A good three minutes seemed to pass before Steel was satisfied enough to turn from the closed door. He ignored Helen crying for her lost doll. Instead, he looked at Rob. 'How many more rhymes has she memorised?'

'I don't know,' said Rob. It was the truth.

Steel looked down at Helen, and Helen looked back up at him, still crying as she held on tightly to Sapphire.

'Keep her with you at all times.'

Sapphire nodded and Steel looked at Rob once more as the crying continued. 'Has she other dolls?'

'Yes.'

'Then find her one,' was Steel's only offering as he moved towards the stairs.

'The way— the way that doll disappeared.' Rob had to ask the question. 'Is that— is that the way that my mother and father . . .?'

'Yes.' Steel stopped halfway down the stairs. 'And you almost went the same way.'

Rob looked at the closed door of the attic room. It was still quiet and the glow from inside the room was still extinguished.

'So, from now on and until I say differently, this floor is out of bounds,' said Steel as he moved on down to the bottom of the stairs.

'But my mother's still in that room.'

Steel's reply came from the landing below. 'Not any more.' And his footsteps could be heard as he began to descend the second flight of stairs.

Rob turned slowly to find Sapphire looking at him. 'But I saw her,' he insisted. 'I saw her in the room.'

Sapphire shook her head.

'I did. I heard her voice.' He remembered the strange light and the shadowy figures and that one familiar figure half seen, only half recognised. And he found, now, out here on the comparatively normal peaceful landing, that he was not completely sure of what he had seen,

41

or what the strange light had wanted him to see.

'It wasn't her?' he asked, tentatively.

Sapphire shook her head once more. Rob held her gaze for a moment, then had to look away, quickly. Helen's crying had stopped but Rob felt tears inside himself. His throat was tight as he tried hard to fight the choked, helpless sensation. He had to fight it. He had no intention of breaking down in front of his sister and this woman called Sapphire. He did not trust her or Steel. Not completely. He accepted her and he was fascinated by her, but he could not trust her. Not yet. And, because of the young, and therefore strange, feelings that he had for her, she would be the last person to see him weep. Perhaps later, in the privacy of his own room, and in his own bed, he would allow himself the painful but necessary luxury of crying.

'Mama's coming home?'

Rob realised that Helen was talking to him. He reached out and touched her, brushed her hair with his fingers. 'Not yet,' he answered.

'Soon?'

Rob looked up at Sapphire and Sapphire nodded.

'Yes,' said Rob to his sister, as Sapphire led them down the dark stairs. 'Soon.'

Chapter Six

Rob was awakened by the sound of hammering. He lifted his head from the pillow and stared around him at the daylight. It seemed a long time since he had last seen it.

The noise of hammering continued. It was coming from above, somewhere on the top floor.

Rob eased himself out from the bed. He pushed his feet into his slippers and pulled his dressing-gown on over his pyjamas. He then moved to the window and looked out.

There was the usual high, pinched sound of the wind, but the day was bright and clear. There was something moving on the water of the bay, moving well out from the jetty at Scars Edge. Rob could see that it was a boat of some kind but he could not determine its direction, not from this distance. Then the boat was lost from view and Rob was reminded of the image he had seen in Helen's room. He turned from the window.

The steady sound of hammering grew louder as Rob came out from his room on the second floor landing. He pulled the door to quietly and looked towards the cupboard-stair. The stair door was closed but the hammering was taking place on the floor above. The attic room floor. The out-of-bounds floor.

Rob walked quietly across the landing and opened the cupboard-stair door very carefully. The hammering sound reverberated on the boxed-in, narrow staircase. Rob closed the door gently, but left it off the catch. He then climbed the stairs cautiously, using his hands and feet to give him balance as he kept his head and body low down and out of sight. He reached the top of the stair, still keeping his head down, then raised it slowly to peer between the attic landing bannisters.

Steel was working with hammer, wood and four-inch nails. Coolly and methodically, he was nailing-up the door of the attic bedroom.

Rob came out from the cupboard-stair, closing the door quietly and carefully once more. He tip-toed across the landing towards the stairs. Then, noticing something, he stopped at the landing window and looked out.

He recognised the vehicle even though it was one-point-nine-four miles away. It was the small, blue and white police car from Scars Edge. Rob watched it dip and bump off the small ferry-boat. Then it disappeared from view for a few moments as it moved down the slope at the side of the causeway. Rob waited and, sure enough, the white roof of Constable Daly's car bobbed up again as it climbed the short incline on to the wooden bridge at the end of the dirt track road. The only road. The approach road to the house.

'Breakfast!' said Sapphire as Rob entered the kitchen parlour. There was food on the table and Helen was already sat there.

'Oh, I'm— I'm not hungry, thanks.' Rob lied, keeping his head turned away, knowing that if he looked Sapphire in the eyes he had no chance of telling a lie, let alone getting away with it.

He moved to the window and looked out, pretending to be looking at nothing more specific than the general view.

'What is it?' Sapphire looked across at him as she put a plate of buttered toast down in front of Helen.

'What?'

'What's out there?'

'Nothing.' Rob decided to give Sapphire at least one quick glance to show that he was behaving normally. 'Just looking at the weather, that's all.'

Sapphire smiled slightly to herself as she turned to the stove.

44

She took boiled eggs from a saucepan and placed them in two egg-cups.

Rob tried to make it sound as convincingly casual as possible. 'Oh, I almost forgot. He wants you. Asked me to tell you.'

'Steel?'

• 'Yes. He's on the top landing.'

Sapphire had probably decided to make the lie easier for Rob. She cracked Helen's egg, set the plate down on the table, then turned back to the stove before asking, 'So what does he want me for?'

'He's not likely to tell me, is he?'

'I suppose not,' Sapphire replied, strictly for Rob's benefit.

If Rob could have tapped the atmosphere, or the mind-waves, or had the insight and the power to avoid looking the subconscious in the eye, he might have got away with it.

'I sent no message.' Steel's voice moved freely and clearly inside Sapphire's head. 'I didn't think you had.' She sent the answer back to him, using the same smooth, silent process. Showing nothing, she poured milk for Helen and smiled at the child as the effortless communication took place.

In contrast, Rob made hard work out of sitting down nonchalantly at the table as Sapphire walked to the door. Once there, she turned back to look at Rob.

'First a wall. Then a room,' she said. It was like a quiet warning. 'You have to trust us, Rob.'

'But I do trust you.' Rob looked at her quickly, then, as a diversion, he reached for the coffee pot. He heard the door close, then looked up quickly. He waited until Sapphire had moved along the hall, until he could hear her climbing the first flight of stairs, then he got up quickly from the table and reached out for Helen's dressing-gown which was flung over the back of her chair.

'Put this on,' he said, quietly but urgently, as he draped the gown across Helen's shoulders.

Helen shrugged the dressing-gown off. 'But I don't want it on.'

Rob grabbed the garment before it fell to the floor. This time he took Helen's free hand and shoved it through the sleeve of the gown. 'I said put it on. Quickly.'

'I'm eating my breakfast.'

Rob took her other arm and Helen transferred the spoon from one hand to the next, still eating her egg as her brother tugged her arm through the sleeve and pulled the gown over her shoulders. He then moved quickly to the window and looked out. There was nothing to be seen yet from this level. But Rob could hear the steady sound of the approaching police car. He hurried back to the table and snatched the spoon from Helen's hand.

'No!' Helen raised her voice but Rob put his finger to his lips.

'Please, Helen,' he pleaded, 'We've got to be ready.'

Still managing to eat her toast, she looked at him, wide-eyed. 'Ready?'

Rob nodded as he lifted her from the chair. 'We're leaving.'

Still staring at him, Helen crunched on her toast. And Rob knelt down to straighten and button her dressing-gown. 'Constable Daly's coming,' he whispered conspiratorially, seeing his sister's eyes widen even more. 'He's coming here, to the house.'

'Are we going with him, Rob?' asked Helen, still munching toast.

'Yes. So hurry.'

And the sound of the car outside, much closer now as it drove slowly and steadily along the rough dirt track.

Rob took Helen's hand and led her to the door.

'Did you tell Sapphire?' Helen asked, putting the last of the toast into her mouth.

'No, I didn't,' said Rob and reached for the handle of the door.

'But she'll be cross.'

Rob opened the kitchen door very carefully.

'You should have told her,' Helen insisted.

Rob peered out into the hallway. There was no-one in the hall or on the stairs. Outside, the car could be heard as it shuddered over the cattle-grid.

Rob looked down at the small figure of his sister. 'They're nailing up the door of your room, Helen,' he told her, but she simply stared back up at him without understanding. 'Nailing it up good and solid. So that no-one can get in and no-one can get out. Is that the right way to bring Mum and Dad back?'

Helen was still staring up at him. But his last words had got through to her. She began to cry quietly and Rob put his arm about her as he opened wide the kitchen door.

'It's alright. The policeman's here,' said Rob, as he led his sister out into the hallway.

Steel and Sapphire had stood at the top landing window and watched the approach of the police car.

'I'm sorry, but the boy just doesn't trust you,' said Sapphire, as she looked out at the long, narrow strip of road.

Steel was unconcerned as he asked, 'Does he trust you?'

'A little.'

'Only you're supposed to be the diplomat, aren't you?'

'Amongst other things, yes . . .'

'The one who's supposed to sweet-talk kids like that.' Steel gazed at the small, blue and white car as it bumped its way along the rough track road. 'Reassure them. Win them over. So that we can get on with this job. Fight this battle.'

Sapphire said nothing. She watched the sunlight flash from the white roof of the car as it dipped and rose again over a bump in the road. As the car clattered over the cattle-grid, Steel pointed at the nailed-up bedroom door. 'Because this is a bad one. It's strong and it's dangerous, and this time it's trying to reason things out, in its own way.'

'What kind of things?' Sapphire glanced towards the door.

'Methods.'

Sapphire looked at him. Outside, the car could be heard slowing as it drew near to the house.

'Go and listen,' said Steel, nodding towards the boarded-up door.

Sapphire walked to the door, put her ear as close to it as she could and listened. Through the door, somewhere in the room,

47

a voice was speaking. It was a flat, monotonous whisper that did not change in pitch, so that what was said sounded almost mechanical.

The flat, dull voice was chanting *'Ring-a-ring o' roses, Ring-a-ring o' roses, Ring-a-ring o' roses.'* Exactly the same words, using the same inflections said over and over again. It was like a looped tape, like a record that had stuck.

Sapphire turned to look at Steel, but he was still gazing out and down from the window. 'That's Time marking Time,' he said, without changing his position at the window.

Down below, outside the house, there was the sound of a car door slamming. 'So the last thing we need right now is someone coming here.' Steel commented. 'Someone who doesn't know, being helped, in turn, by someone who doesn't understand.'

He listened to, but did not seem perturbed by, the sound of footsteps approaching the house. 'Think you can handle that policeman?' he asked, as he turned from the window.

'Yes,' said Sapphire, confidently, and followed Steel down the attic stairs.

Rob could hear the slow, measured footsteps of Constable Daly walking towards the front door of the house. The policeman walked on gravel. Soon he would reach the flagstones and it was then only ten or twelve yards to the front door itself.

The top bolt had been easy to slide back. The lower one, though, was proving difficult. Rob wanted to open the door without being heard from inside the house. He then planned to bundle Helen outside as quickly as possible. Just run to the policeman, that was all they had to do. Then Constable Daly could ask his questions, making sure that he got straightforward, sensible answers. Steel and Sapphire would have to explain things. After all, they were only people. They weren't the police. Once they saw that uniform and the notebook, they would have to stop doing things their way. In fact, Rob was quite looking forward to seeing how the cool, immovable Steel would react when he was confronted by proper authority.

Rob tugged at the bolt. It slid back with what seemed a loud, grating sound.

He looked up and round, but there was no-one on the stairs There was only Helen, standing waiting with him at the door. Outside, the footsteps were now treading the flagstones. Rob was reaching for the door-catch when he saw Helen looking towards the first staircase. He turned quickly.

Sapphire and Steel were standing on the stair. They seemed quite calm and relaxed as they watched Rob and Helen.

'I— I have to do it.' Rob found himself already apologising.

'Then do it,' said Sapphire.

Rob stared at her. He expected some kind of panic. A struggle even. Not this degree of calmness. 'It's my home. I live here. I have to do it, have to tell— someone else.'

The footsteps scraped to a halt at the other side of the front door.

'Are you speaking for both of you?' asked Sapphire.

'Of course I am.' As Rob spoke, there was a loud knocking on the door. And a quick thought passed through Rob's mind. The thought was that he was hearing an irregular knock. An everyday knock. A normal one.

'I don't think you *can* speak for both of you.' Sapphire smiled the bright smile and reached out a hand. 'Come on, Helen.'

Helen looked at Rob only once. She then walked straight to the staircase. As the door was knocked upon a second time, Helen climbed the first two steps and held out her hand to take Sapphire's.

Rob felt a little hurt and betrayed. But then, Helen was six, she could be easily influenced. He reached out for the door-catch. 'I'm still going to do it. I'm going to tell him everything.'

'And do you think he'll listen?'

'Of course he'll listen. That policeman knows me.'

Sapphire was still smiling. 'Go on, then. Try to tell him.'

Rob reached forward quickly while the decision was still his to make. He unlocked the door-catch. For a split second, as he

4

did this, he somehow sensed something, as if from the corner of his mind. It seemed as if there was a quick surge of brightness and blueness from the direction of the stairs, from where Sapphire's eyes would be.

Rob dragged the door open wide.

Constable Daly was young and friendly, pleasant and reliable. He took off his peaked cap as he stepped through the doorway. 'Hallo, Rob,' he said, as he entered.

Then, as Rob found himself opening the door yet again, Daly was taking off his cap once more and stepping through the doorway. 'Hallo, Rob,' he said, and entered the house a second time.

Then the whole procedure happened a third time. When it happened the fourth time, Rob found that he was somehow set back from the doorway. He could actually see himself opening the door.

'Hallo, Rob.' Daly was still removing his cap and stepping through the doorway.

'I can make that happen for as long as necessary.'

Rob turned at the sound of Sapphire's voice, even though this other version of him, this image, continued to open the door to the constable. 'Hallo, Rob.' And yet again. 'Hallo, Rob.'

'For as long as it takes to prevent you from talking to him,' Sapphire added, still smiling. 'And that could be ages. So be fair. I'm sure the poor man has better things to do.'

'Hallo, Rob.' It was perpetual. Like a dummy figure in an amusement arcade, that uttered the same words, smiled the same fixed smile and made the same predictable moves, over and over forever, or until the machinery was worn out.

After the eighth or ninth cycle had been completed, Constable Daly no longer resembled a human being, let alone a candidate for sanity and authority.

'Hallo, Rob.'

'But how did you do it?'

Rob and Helen were back in the kitchen again with

Sapphire. Constable Daly had driven back to Scars Edge. He looked slightly puzzled, in the way that people do when they feel that they have been somewhere, or done something before, perhaps in a dream. But he had left feeling satisfied. Rob had watched, without being able to say a word, as Steel moved into action. He had literally stepped into Daly's arrival at the door, like a fair-owner stepping on to a moving roundabout. Therefore it became Steel, not Rob, who had opened the door, Steel who had asked Daly what he wanted, who told the policeman that everything was alright at that house, and that he, Steel, was a friend of the family who was visiting, in the hope of some peace and quiet in the country.

When the front door had been closed again and Daly was on his way back to the car, Rob had threatened to climb out of a window and run after him. But Sapphire's counter-threat had made him change his mind. She had said that if he did that, she would make sure that he spent the next few hours climbing through the window, over and over again, but getting nowhere.

'It doesn't really matter how I did it,' said Sapphire, setting out a newly cooked egg for Helen.

'It does,' insisted Rob. 'If you can make Time go backwards . . .'

'Who said I can?'

'You just did it. Out in the hall. And last night, when you kept changing into different clothes.'

'The changing of clothes was an illusion,' she told him. 'They were things I'd worn in the past. I was projecting an image for you, that's all.'

'But out there in the hall . . .' Rob followed her as she crossed the room and began to straighten the larder cupboard. 'That wasn't an illusion was it?'

'No.' And that was all she seemed prepared to say as she closed the larder door and moved back to Helen and the table.

Rob pursued it. 'That was Time. You were making Time go back.'

Sapphire said nothing as she began to clear the kitchen table.

'So why can't you make it go back twenty-four hours? Why can't you take it back to just before yesterday? To when our parents were still here?'

Sapphire looked up slowly from the table. 'Don't you think I would have done that already,' she asked, 'If I was able to?'

Rob thought about it. He remembered the sick fear that he had felt in the attic bedroom, and the tense, serious faces of Sapphire and Steel as they fought and held back whatever it was that had invaded that room.

Sapphire appeared to have interpreted his thoughts yet again. 'First a wall. Then a room,' she said. 'What next? A house? A road? A village? A town? Then what?'

Rob stared at her.

'Look, I haven't the power to take Time back twenty-four hours.' Having read his thoughts, Sapphire now seemed prepared to give some explanations. 'I cannot take it back that far.' She demonstrated with her hand. 'Imagine a rubber ball bounced on the floor here.'

Helen moved her head up and down, as if watching an invisible ball.

'The ball hitting the floor the first time is the incident. The bouncing that follows is the echo. The momentum. I'm just able to keep that momentum going for a little while longer, that's all.'

Sapphire then gave Rob a quick glint of the smile as she turned and began to remove the cloth from the kitchen table.

'Does anyone have the power to take Time back further?' Rob had to know.

Sapphire began to shake and fold the table-cloth. 'Something does, in a way yes.'

'Some*thing*? Not someone?'

Sapphire nodded. 'In it's own way, yes.'

'You mean whatever's in that corridor? Whatever it was that came into Helen's room? That came and . . .?'

And he stopped because Sapphire had turned to look at him. Her face was serious. There was no hint of the smile there. 'It has access to all kinds of power,' she said, 'When it's encouraged.'

52

Rob waited for her to say more. But Sapphire had turned away. She reached down and lifted Helen from the chair.

Rob walked idly to the door and out into the hallway. There was no point in running, he thought. He might just as well try running on the spot.

He moved to the window, rested his elbows upon the ledge and looked out. He could not see much from this viewpoint. There was a dip in the terrain, a hundred yards or so past the cattle-grid, which cut off the view to Deadman's Point and the bay. A string of decayed, wooden fences crossed the skyline. Whenever the wind blew at something near gale force, the loose fencing would rattle violently and break away. Rob had heard one piece bowling along the rough track road one night, making a noise like a football rattle. And Rob remembered, now, how his father was always planning to go out with an axe and a barrow and chop down all the fencing to use for firewood.

Rob moved from the window and wandered along to the foot of the stairs. He looked up at the staircase that was now bright with cold sunlight. Thinking of the nailed-up door, he tried to see if he could imagine the strange light and the images now, during the daytime. He found that he could and the thought made him shiver slightly.

Still looking up at the stairs, he remembered Sapphire's last words to him: 'when it's encouraged,' and wondered what she had meant by that.

Chapter Seven

Steel appeared during the evening. He had spent most of the day examining both the inside and the outside of the house.

Helen had fallen asleep on the couch in the sitting room. Sapphire covered her with a blanket and decided to leave her there for the time being.

With the blustery darkness outside and the lamplight and shadows within the house, Rob was anxious to stay in the kitchen where it was bright and warm. He was hurrying along the hallway, towards the kitchen, when Steel loomed out from the open cellar doorway, startling Rob in the process.

'Would you happen to know which room in the house is the youngest?' Steel asked as he closed the cellar door.

When Rob had eventually worked out what Steel had meant, he told the man that his father had had the small office extension, that adjoined the kitchen, built the year before.

Sapphire and Steel examined just about every item in the office, he with his eyes, she with her hands. Sapphire touched pieces of furniture, ornaments and items of office equipment. Each time she touched, she 'sensed' and gave approximate dates of manufacture. Even if the object was new, she could determine the age of any recycled elements that were part of the structure of that object.

Rob watched them, fascinated. The 'youngest' room in the house! Rob smiled to himself as he thought. Here these two were, conducting the kind of inventory that would put any book-keeper or accountant to shame, and Steel had to use the wrong word, ask which room was the 'youngest'.

'We're clearing the lot.'

Rob was jolted out of his thoughts by Steel's voice.

'Put it all in the cellar. I need an empty room to work from.'

Steel began to shift the contents of the office into the small lobby that divided the office from the kitchen. Rob was left with the hardest job, humping each piece from the kitchen and down into the cellar. After his third cellar trip, Rob stopped in the kitchen for a moment to get his breath back.

Steel appeared in the office lobby with an upright chair.

'You know when you had this job on a ship?' Rob began, curious.

'What ship?' Steel did not seem in the mood for questions as he turned back into the office doorway.

'Sapphire said you had an assignment once, on a ship.'

Steel halted in the office doorway. He glanced at Sapphire as she eased past him with some books and moved into the kitchen.

'What happened?' Rob was still anxious to know.

'We sank the ship, for its own good,' said Steel, indifferently. 'So consider yourself lucky.'

'Lucky?' asked Rob.

'Yes.' Steel turned and walked back into the office, saying 'It's not as easy to sink a house.'

Rob glanced at Sapphire, but Sapphire, with a slight smile on her face, had turned away with the books.

Deciding that he would not ask any more questions if it meant that Steel might possibly make a fool out of him, Rob picked up the chair and half carried, half dragged it, across the kitchen, out into the hallway and then on to the cellar steps. But, when he returned to the kitchen, he found that he was still curious to know. And why not? He lived here. It affected him.

'What was the trigger?'

Sapphire looked up as Rob re-entered the kitchen.

'Which trigger?' she asked.

'Well, when you said that Time had tried to break through, up in Helen's room, you said there was a trigger, a final ingredient that made it happen.'

'That's right.'

'Well, what was the trigger, the final ingredient, on that ship?'

Sapphire was checking the contents of each book. 'An out-of-date ship's log,' she said, without looking up from her work. 'The captain had a weakness for nautical souvenirs.'

'Oh.' Rob wandered back to the office doorway. He could hear Steel clattering about inside the office and there were some more bits and pieces stacked in the doorway waiting to be shifted.

Rob sighed, picked up a desk-lamp and a filing-tray and walked back across the kitchen. A thought occurred to him as he passed the busy-looking Sapphire.

'Not so silly then, are they?' he said as he walked to the door.

'Who?' Sapphire was still flicking through the pages of each book, checking the text and each illustration.

Rob decided he would not make it a question this time. It was an observation. Anyway, he was tired of asking questions and being made to wait for the answers.

'These things that are trying to break through the Time fabric.' He eased the kitchen door open with his foot. 'A ship's log at sea. A nursery-rhyme in a child's room. No, they're not so silly.' He began to ease himself and the objects through the gap of the open door. 'Sounds to me as if those things know what they're doing.'

Sapphire looked up slowly from the books. Out in the hall, the cellar door clattered open as Rob pushed it and began to whistle his way down the cellar steps.

Without him realising it, Rob's observation had been dead on target. Steel saw the thoughtful look on Sapphire's face as he came out through the office lobby.

'What's wrong?' he asked her.

'I'm not sure. Just something the boy said. It reminded me of something that you said earlier.' Sapphire closed the last of the books. 'When you spoke of methods being used.'

It had taken almost three hours to clear the office, to free it from the many possible ingredients and triggers that might be hidden in the room. Rob thought that it looked more like a cell as he carried the very last item out into the kitchen. And he wondered what his father would think if he could see his office now.

Sapphire and Steel were still in the empty office, so Rob tried his usual whistle accompaniment as he made his way down the stone steps and into the darkness of the cellar, where the whistling seemed to echo under the old brick and stone support arches.

When he had climbed back up the cellar steps, Rob switched the light off and closed the cellar door with a certain amount of relief. Feeling tired after the hard work, he glanced at the nearest clock which, like all the others, was now working again, and saw that it was twenty-five to ten. He began walking back towards the kitchen when he heard the voice.

'Ro-ob!'

It called out to him, faintly. Rob stopped and turned and listened, not quite sure, at first, whether he had heard his name called or not.

Then the faint voice called again. 'Ro-ob!'

Rob thought that he recognised it this time. It sounded like the voice of his mother. And it was calling from upstairs somewhere. Rob turned his head and looked up with a slight feeling of uncertainty. His first thought was to go and tell Sapphire and Steel. But then it was his own mother's voice that he heard, *if* he had heard it. And she didn't sound at all alarmed or concerned.

He listened, but the voice had stopped. Rob glanced towards the kitchen, then turned and walked slowly along to the bottom of the dark stair. He placed his foot on the first step, then looked up at the stairs and listened.

A moment or two passed. Nothing. Rob was about to turn back down the hallway.

'Ro-ob!'

He turned around again quickly. The voice had been faint but much clearer this time, as if it had been calling out to him quietly. But he was sure of one thing now. It was definitely his mother's voice.

Rob began to climb the stairs.

Up at the top of the house, on the attic landing, the light remained switched off. But the darkness was lit, just slightly, by a faint glow that shimmered and danced around the edges of the closed attic bedroom door. Fine, thin pencil beams that flickered and reflected upon the strong wood that criss-crossed the sealed-up door.

There was a creaking of the stairs from below as Rob climbed them, and at that, the glow went out from behind the attic room door, leaving the small landing in complete darkness.

Rob was climbing the second flight of stairs which was lit by small, ornate wall-lamps. He reached the landing, and stopped. 'Mum!' he called, quietly. He listened but there was no reply. He tried again. 'Mum!'

'Up here, Rob.'

Rob turned his head quickly to look. The quiet voice had come from the attic floor somewhere. His first thought, an impulsive one, was that she could be in danger. So he didn't stop to think of Sapphire's warning as he moved across to the cupboard-stair door and opened it.

The attic stairs were in total darkness. So, too, was the landing above. Rob tried the light switch. It did not work. He opened the stair door wide and then saw that the staircase bulb had been taken. Probably by Steel.

'Where are you, Mum?' he called out to the dark landing above him. A moment or two passed, and then . . .

'Up here, of course.' The voice sounded much closer now. And Rob felt the choked glad tears in his throat. He ignored the darkness as he scrambled up the attic stairs.

When he reached the top he peered around him in the darkness. There was no-one on the landing. And the only door was the one to the attic bedroom. Rob groped his way across the landing and reached out for the door. His hands touched the firm coarse slats of wood. The attic room was still securely boarded-up.

It made no sense, Rob's mind told him, and a sudden feeling of fear surged through him. 'Mum?' he called out, nervously.

His mother's voice came from behind the door of the sealed

room. The voice sounded irritated, puzzled and exasperated. In fact, the right temperament for a home-loving parent who had found herself locked in a room.

'Just what on earth is going on, Rob?' the voice said.

And Rob breathed out as the fear and tension lifted. It was right, it was normal, it was his mother. No-one else could say it like that. 'Mum!' he cried out. 'Oh, Mum!'

'Will you open this door at once, please?' The voice demanded, impatiently.

'Of course.' And then Rob realised. 'Oh, I forgot— it's nailed up.'

'Nailed up? What do you mean, nailed up? Just what have you been doing, Rob?'

'Mum, look, let me explain . . .'

'You can explain when I'm out of this room.' Rob's mother's voice was angry now. 'So just open the door, will you? Right now.'

'I will, Mum. Honest.' He decided that it was the wrong time to try to explain. 'Just wait,' he said, turning from the door. 'I'll fetch Steel and Sapphire.'

'There's no need to fetch them.'

Rob was making his way back to the staircase when he realised just what had been said. It reached him like a kind of afterthought, causing the fear and uncertainty to flood back. He could not really understand it or explain it, even to himself. It was just that something seemed not quite right, seemed slightly off-centre.

He turned slowly to face the door and asked, 'How do you know them?'

'Know who?' the voice asked, innocently.

'Sapphire and Steel. How can you possibly know them?'

There was no answer for a moment or two, as if beyond the door, this problem was being worked out.

Rob's mother's voice eventually spoke again. 'Well, whoever they are— I don't know— friends of yours, I suppose. I don't exactly know them.' Then, sharper, 'Now please open this door.'

Rob would never know why he walked slowly back to the

dark doorway. It was not just the strict voice of his mother that made him. It was something else. Like the feeling of alarm and uncertainty, it was something that he could not quite understand and never would. It was as if he was drawn towards the door. As if the door and the room beyond it and whatever was in that room were his only concern. Nothing else mattered. And, strangely enough, not even his mother seemed to really matter. Only the door, this nailed and boarded door was important. That was his main objective.

'But I can't open the door without help,' he found himself saying, as his body was willed towards the door.

'Of course you can. It's very simple.' His mother's voice had changed its approach. Now it was good-humoured and coaxing. 'Just kneel down by the door, Rob. Just outside the door.'

Rob knelt slowly down.

'Close to the door,' the voice insisted, as if it could see him through the wood-work. 'Put your face close to the door.'

Rob shuffled forward on his knees.

'I mean, it's easy enough to open the door,' the voice continued to cajole him. 'Easy enough to let us out.'

Rob reached the door on his knees. He now found that he was pressing his face against the rough bars of wood. There was the smell of pine and his mind raced. It saw the wind-blown fencing and the piece that flew and cartwheeled along the road, and his father walking, dressed in heavy coat and boots, head-down against the wind.

'That's it, Rob. That's it,' the voice sounded pleased. 'Now all you have to do is say a rhyme. A nursery-rhyme. Any one, it doesn't matter, just as long as it's old. Can you remember one?'

Still confused, still kneeling at the door, Rob nodded his head. His face rubbed against the surface of the wood.

'Then say it, Rob.'

But, in Rob's mixed-up mind there were not rhymes, only a few random words and fragmented pictures.

The voice continued, coaxing, almost wheedling. 'Because most nursery-rhymes are a part of history, Rob.' The voice rambled on. 'And I've always taught you that, haven't I, Rob?'

Then, before Rob could answer. 'So say the one that's in your head. The one that's in there now.'

And, through the haziness of Rob's mind, a rhyme appeared. It was crystal-clear and could well have been printed there in his head.

'Think of the soldiers,' chattered the voice. 'Climbing stairs, swords in their hands. Searching for people.' Then loud, like a shrill command. 'Say it!'

'*Goosey, goosey gander . . .*' Rob began.

'That's the one,' whispered the voice and the glow flickered faintly around the edge of the door.

'*Where shall I . . .?*'

'*Whither shall I?*'

'*Whither shall I wander . . .?*'

'That's it,' the voice whispered encouragingly.

'*Upstairs and downstairs . . .*' Rob stopped. He could hear the low, familiar rumbling sound. There were also other sounds. Heavy footsteps climbing the attic stairs. The jingle of metal.

'All of it, Rob,' pleaded the voice. 'Say all of it.'

Perhaps the room had gone too far. Or perhaps it had simply underestimated Rob. But something, some tiny scrap of spirit remained of his senses.

Two cloaked and helmeted figures were climbing the stairs. Each one had a drawn sword in his hand. The glow pulsated around the edges of the door, highlighting the metal of the swords, breastplates, helmets and buckles.

'All of it, Rob,' begged the voice from the room. 'Say it. Say the rest of the rhyme.'

But that tiny fragment of spirit made Rob turn to look. The figures had reached the landing. They loomed high above him. They were dressed in the uniforms of Ironside troopers but, to Rob, they were hardly human. In the semi-darkness their figures were thin and gaunt, and their faces were skull-like under the visors of the helmets.

The troopers strode across the floor towards Rob and the attic room door. They appeared to pass not just through him, but above him, as a train might pass over a camera that is set between railway lines. And, as they passed him, without once looking at him, Rob could smell oldness, the smell of another time.

And the attic room door appeared to change in that fraction of a second that the troopers passed him. It was like an old-fashioned door in a cottage. One trooper flanked the door, the other raised his sword and began to break the door open.

'No!' shouted Rob loudly, as his mind cleared and his senses streamed back. He scrambled quickly to his feet and clambered down the attic stairs, as fast as the steep steps would allow.

The moment Rob shouted, the troopers vanished and the boarded-up attic room door reappeared. But Rob, in his flight, had no time to see these things.

Neither did he see the dancing glow of light as it moved downwards and became a solitary pool of light at the bottom of the door. The glow appeared to flare up, just briefly. It then died out, leaving only darkness behind the door. But a small patch of light seemed to have separated itself. It eased out from under the door and moved on to the landing. It then stopped.

The patch of light was not very bright. Neither was it very large. About eight inches in diameter, it resembled the sun's reflection from something like a small hand mirror. But this was more than a reflection. It stayed still on the landing for a moment, as Rob hurried down the stairs below. The patch of light then began to move, almost leisurely, across the landing. As it moved, it made a faint, rumbling, fabric sound. It reached the top of the attic stairs and proceeded to slide, like mercury might, over the ridge of the landing and on to the first step. It paused for a moment, as if listening, and its sound ceased.

Then the very faint, almost imperceptible sound started up again as the patch of light began to descend the attic stairs.

Chapter Eight

Some of the clocks had stopped again. Those from the second landing upwards.

The patch of light had found its way as far as the second landing. Once there, it had heard the voices from below and then hidden itself. It had moved to a corner of the landing, then slid beneath the drugget rug, which hid its pale luminous glow.

By the time Steel, Sapphire and Rob had reached the second landing, all that seemed wrong were the clocks that had stopped on that particular floor.

Steel crossed the landing, opened the cupboard-stair door and looked up into the darkness.

'And it called to you?' he asked.

'Yes,' said Rob. 'It called my name. Called me by my first name.'

Steel moved back from the cupboard-stair. He had carried with him one of the small clocks from the kitchen. He glanced at the clock face. It was the correct time and the clock still worked even though those on the landing were still.

'I thought it was my mother at first.' Rob told the business-like Steel. 'It was her voice. I mean, I wouldn't have gone up there if it wasn't her voice, now would I?'

'Did you see her?' asked Sapphire.

Rob shook his head.

'And these soldiers,' Steel moved about the landing, studying the ceiling and the walls. 'Did they come out from the attic room?'

'No,' said Rob. 'They came up the stairs. Came from down here somewhere.'

Steel looked at Sapphire. She moved to the cupboard-stair, looked at it, then began making what seemed like mental measurements of the landing area. 'A visual refraction could have been let loose during that first breakthrough,' was her first suggestion.

Rob stared at her. 'Visual refraction?'

'You'd probably call them ghosts.'

Before Rob could react, Steel had turned to him. Did *anything* come out from the room?'

'No. Nothing.'

'You're sure?'

'Yes. I'm sure.'

Steel walked to the cupboard-stair door and began to climb the stairs.

'Anyway, it became a different door,' he called after Steel. 'So something could have got out. Those soldiers smashed the door.'

Sapphire moved past him and followed Steel up the attic stairs. She stopped suddenly about three steps up.

'There's something,' said Sapphire. 'I'm not sure what. Just something here somewhere.'

Steel moved back down the stairs. He held out the clock. Rob watched him as he moved it around in the air like some kind of geigercounter.

Sapphire waited until Steel had made a careful study of the clock's face. 'It's still working?'

Steel nodded. 'Yes. Except that it's lost ten minutes.'

'Since we came up these stairs?'

'I think so. Yes.'

'Well,' Sapphire looked at the stairs. 'If the images of the soldiers appeared about here . . .'

'They did,' Rob broke in, pointing to a spot two thirds of the way up the stairs. 'That's where I first saw them.'

Moving up to the point on the stairs, Sapphire looked back at Steel. 'Then that could account for it,' she said, indicating the clock.

Steel gave a kind of impartial nod, eased past her and walked on up the stairs.

As Steel climbed the attic stairs, so the patch of dull light moved out from under the rug on the second landing. Accompanied by its faint murmuring sound, it glided in the other direction, across the landing, and began to descend the stairs to the first landing below.

When Rob reached the landing, staying wisely at the heels of Sapphire and Steel on the way up, he looked first at the attic door.

'It's back as it was,' he exclaimed.

Steel was peering at the clock face. 'And so is the clock.' He held it out in the darkness for Sapphire to see. 'It's at the correct time again.'

Rob began, 'You mean it lost ten minutes just on . . .?'

'Quiet.' Steel raised his hand as he moved to the boarded-up door. He then put his ear close to the wooden struts, and listened. 'Well, one thing's changed,' he said, eventually.

Sapphire took his place at the door and Rob moved with her to listen. From within the room, the flat, mechanical-like whisper, that did not vary in pitch, was saying the words, *'Upstairs and downstairs, Upstairs and downstairs,'* repeatedly.

Sapphire turned her head to look at Rob. 'When your mother's voice called to you . . .'

'That isn't my mother's voice.'

'I know.' Sapphire smiled patiently. 'But when her voice spoke to you, was that the rhyme you chose?'

'I didn't exactly choose it. It was put in my head . . .'

'But was that the rhyme?'

Rob put his head to the door and listened a second time.

'If it is, just tell me.' Sapphire's smile had gone. 'Whatever you do, don't say any of it aloud.'

Rob nodded as he listened. He then looked away from the door. 'That's the one,' he said.

'And did you complete it? Did you say all of it?'

'No.'

Then he heard the other sounds again. Heavy footsteps and

5

the hard jingle of metal as the troopers stamped their way up the stairs. He turned quickly to see if Sapphire and Steel had also heard it. They had.

With swords drawn, the shadowy figures of the Ironside troopers climbed the stairs in exactly the same way as before. To Rob, it was like seeing the repeat of a piece of film.

'Stay as you are,' was the command from Steel.

Rob tried to move closer to him and Sapphire as the troopers marched their way up the stairs.

'Stay just as you are. Don't move!'

Rob stayed as he was.

The troopers reached the landing and advanced across it as before. Rob saw, rather than felt them pass him. There was the stale, musty smell, the skull-like faces under the visors, eyes staring ahead at the door of the room. And the door was the old door once more. The troopers moved to it, one raising his sword to strike the door. Then the figures disappeared and the attic door returned to normal.

Rob was not surprised to find that Steel and Sapphire had taken the incident quite calmly. Even though he could never understand the two of them, at least he was getting used to their unpredictable behaviour. He often felt that, given a few years with this pair, there would be no real surprises left in life.

'That's what you saw before?' Steel was asking him.

'Yes.'

'Any variation.'

'What?' queried Rob.

'Did they seem different this time? Did they act differently?'

'No,' said Rob.

'If he only said a piece of the rhyme,' suggested Sapphire. 'It could have set off a recurring image.'

Steel held out the clock for Sapphire to see. 'It didn't stop,' he said. 'It didn't lose time. Those images didn't affect it.'

'But something did,' said Sapphire as Steel began to descend the stairs, holding the clock out before him.

'Yes. Something did.' Steel reached the place on the stairs where the troopers had first appeared. He swung the clock slowly around, testing the area of stair. The clock continued to tick. 'So those ten minutes were not lost on these stairs.' Steel stepped down to the bottom of the stairs and pushed the cupboard-stair door open wide. 'They were lost on this landing.'

The patch of light waited below on the first landing. It waited by the skirting board, beside the earthenware jar that was neatly arranged with pampasgrass and dried wild flowers.

On the wall, above the earthenware jar, was a framed picture. It was one of many pictures, paintings and prints that Rob's parents had collected and hung on the walls of the house. This particular picture was of an old, seventeenth-century dwelling. It was a small thatched cottage with a cluster of rickety outbuildings. The picture had always fascinated Rob because it was not the usual pretty, thatched cottage. This building looked uncared for, unloved. Because of that, it seemed somehow forbidding. When he first saw it, Rob had thought that it was a painting of a derelict cottage until he noticed the small chimney and its thin spiral of smoke.

While Steel, Sapphire and Rob examined the landing above, and Helen slept soundly in the room below, the patch of light began to move once more. But this time it moved back to the wall and began to climb it. Gliding smoothly over the skirting board, and emitting the low, strange sound, the patch of light skimmed slowly upwards, over the surface of the wall. It reached the picture and slipped behind the wooden frame. The glow was extinguished and the sound died.

Steel had examined the second floor landing but had found nothing. The clock had not stopped on this occasion, neither had it lost any more time.

As Steel led the way down the second flight of stairs, he asked Sapphire about the significance of the second nursery-rhyme.

'Like the first rhyme, this one has historical roots,' Sapphire explained. 'From the Civil War.'

'Civil War?' Steel inquired as he continued to lead the small party down the stairs.

'Yes.' Sapphire continued with her explanation. 'When Parliament troops searched houses, looking for people who wouldn't pray.'

'Wouldn't pray?'

'Unbelievers.'

'Oh,' said Steel, appearing to lose interest in the topic.

'Don't you know your history?' Rob chipped in.

Steel did not bother to look at him. 'I know *mine*, yes,' he said, giving Rob yet another thought to puzzle over.

'But then, it doesn't make sense.' Sapphire said as they reached the second landing.

Steel halted at the foot of the stairs. 'What doesn't make sense?'

'Well, those soldiers are an anachronism. If they're ghosts, they must have lived and died a good hundred years before this house was built.'

Steel looked at her. 'So?'

'So why should they be breaking down a door that was never a part of this house?'

Steel had no idea. He shook his head.

'It's history gone wrong,' said Sapphire, looking back up at the stairs. 'Either that or part of a plan?'

'A plan?' asked Rob, intrigued.

But Sapphire ignored him as she looked back at Steel. 'A deliberate confusion. A way of diverting us.'

'From what?' Steel walked across the landing towards the first flight of stairs, with Rob close behind him.

Sapphire remained on the landing. 'I don't know. But they know it's us. They're not likely to use tricks that we already know, are they?'

Steel passed the picture. 'I doubt it,' he said as he began to descend the first flight of stairs. Rob followed him. He still felt tired, but he did not fancy sleeping in his own bedroom. Not at the moment. He passed the picture, thinking that there was another couch in the sitting room. Maybe if he fell asleep on that, or even pretended to sleep on it, Sapphire might make him a bed there and tuck him up for the night. He was even wondering, though he would never admit it, what a kiss goodnight from Sapphire would be like.

He was still thinking about that imaginary kiss when he almost bumped into Steel, who had stopped on the stairs. Steel was staring at the face of the clock that he held.

'It's lost time again,' he exclaimed. 'Another ten minutes.'

Rob peered over Steel's arm at the clockface as Sapphire hurried across the landing. 'Then it must have been lost right here,' she said, pointing at the landing. She passed the picture but it was too late, even though she saw the glow from the corner of her eye and turned her head quickly to look.

She heard the faint sound and saw the patch of light glowing through the painted, ramshackle cottage.

'Steel!' she cried out.

Rob and Steel turned quickly from the clock. They stared back at the landing and Rob's mouth opened in shock and amazement.

There was no-one on the landing.

Chapter Nine

Steel made no immediate move back on to the landing. He stood at the top of the first flight of stairs and took a careful look at the landing area. Rob noticed that there was no surprise on the man's face, only the look of calm determination that was always there whenever he was confronted by a difficult and dangerous problem. And it seemed as if this particular problem was of a kind that he was used to, that he might possibly have experienced before. Once more, he was like an expert examining a minefield before attempting to cross it.

Eventually, he called out quietly to the empty landing. 'Sapphire?'

There was no reply.

Rob looked at the landing, looked at all the familiar objects that once symbolised home. The decorative table, the putty-coloured earthenware jar, the dried plants, the painting of the tumbledown cottage.

'Sapphire?' Steel called out a second time, and there was a trace of urgency in his voice now.

'Yes, Steel?' Sapphire's voice seemed so close at hand that Rob was almost startled by it.

'Just tell me.' Steel lowered his head in concentration, to listen rather than to watch.

'I'm in a room. A tiny room,' said Sapphire's voice from the deserted landing.

'Sitting, standing, what?'

'Standing.'

'*Where* are you standing?'

'Facing a wall. Just a blank piece of wall. It's an old wall. Old plaster. Beams. It's very old.'

'In this house? Rob's house?'

'No.' And there was just the slightest tremor in Sapphire's voice. Rob heard it. He looked at Steel, but Steel was still listening hard, still concentrating.

'You haven't changed your position?'

'No,' replied the unseen Sapphire. 'I'm standing exactly as I was when I was last in the house with you.'

Steel raised his head quickly. 'You're still in the house, Sapphire.'

'Yes, Steel.'

'Keep remembering that.' He looked hard at the landing now. 'And don't change that position. Don't move at all. Don't make yourself a part of that room. Do you understand?'

'Yes, Steel.' Sapphire's voice said, with a slight exclamation, like annoyance, like self-reproach. 'We walked right into it, didn't we? I walked into it.' And Rob sensed the touch of nervousness in that voice and it worried him.

'Don't think of that. You're still in the house.' Steel raised his voice as he drove home the warning. 'Remember that you're still in this house with us. Right?'

There was no answer.

'Sapphire?'

The reply was only a second or two late but, to Rob, the emptiness of the landing made it seem interminable. 'Yes, I heard that, Steel,' said the trapped voice.

'Good.' Steel seemed to relax slightly. He then looked up at the landing space once more. 'Now, from where you stand, describe that room to me.'

'It's a— well, it's like part of an old cottage.' Sapphire's voice said from the landing of the house. 'A scullery. Yes, a scullery. A scullery in an old cottage. Not a— not a very tidy place. It seems a bit ramshackle.'

Her words reminded Rob vaguely of the picture. He was about to glance up and across at it when Steel spoke again.

'Night or day?'

'Day.' Sapphire's voice came quickly back at him.

'Well, just remember that you're in Rob's house with us, and that it's night.'

71

'Yes.'

'Just think of that room as a picture.' Steel continued, 'Just a picture. Nothing real. A picture that you're looking at . . .'

'It was a picture.'

'What?' Steel stared at the landing, stared in the direction of Sapphire's voice.

'A picture on the landing. That's what I was looking at when it happened. Left side, almost at the top of the stairs. See it?'

Steel saw it. So did Rob. There was no glow to be seen. Just an ordinary, innocent looking painting of an old dilapidated cottage.

'Yes, I see it, said Steel.

'Well something was waiting for us.' Sapphire's voice spoke out from the vacant landing. 'It got into the picture and it wants me to be in there, too. It wants me to think that I'm in the scullery of that cottage.'

Steel spoke sharply. 'Well you're not.'

'No.' Then, like a shiver. 'It's cold here . . .'

'You're not in that room.' Steel raised his voice, still sharp. It was almost a shout.

When Sapphire's voice spoke again, it was quieter but there was still the hesitant tone to it. 'Sorry, Steel.' Then a pause, and Rob looked at the picture and imagined the small, cheerless room in the cottage that seemed somehow so uninviting, and he found that he could also imagine Sapphire's feeling of coldness. He was almost sharing it with her. He rubbed at his arms and shivered as his eyes remained fixed on the picture.

And, as he looked, Sapphire spoke again. 'It's just that— well, it's just that something happened in this— in that room once. Something terrible. It knows that. It wants me to sense it. Wants me to know. Wants me to be a part of this room, a part of what happened here.'

As Sapphire spoke, Rob found that his eyes and his mind were concentrating on one small window in the picture. One tiny lattice window in what looked like an attached outhouse. The projection was of stone and had a sloping tiled roof that was overgrown with briars.

'Sapphire!'

'It's alright,' she called back, re-assuring Steel. I'm in control of my mind. I won't think what it wants me to think.'

'That's fine. Because you're only a few feet away from us,' Steel reminded her. 'Just a few feet away, on the landing in Rob's house.'

'Yes.'

Steel paused for a moment and then took up a position on the top stair, as close to the landing as he dared. 'Now, Sapphire, when I tell you, look to your left, to where the picture is. Do it very quickly, then back as you are. Do you understand?'

'Yes, I understand,' came the reply.

'I want to know if you can still see the picture. But don't forget, look very quickly then back.' Steel waited a moment. 'Now,' he called.

There was an uneasy silence as Rob and Steel waited.

Steel broke the silence. 'Sapphire?'

'It's— it's alright.' But there was the hesitation again in Sapphire's voice. 'The picture isn't there.' And then she added quickly, in what seemed like a rush of words. 'There's a rope instead. A rope hanging on the wall. And a hook. And— and some kind of block with an axe in it. A chopping-block, I suppose. There's some logs and pieces of firewood lying around . . .'

Steel interrupted her. 'Are you looking towards us again, Sapphire?'

'Yes.'

'Then forget what you've seen. It doesn't belong here.'

'No.'

'And just stay as you are.' Steel turned on the stairs and walked down three or four steps. He stood there, in thought, his back turned to the landing.

Rob looked down the stairs. 'Couldn't we get the picture?' he whispered. 'Reach out and get the picture. Wouldn't that stop it?'

'Whoever tried to get the picture would be in that room with her,' Steel said, without turning.

Sapphire's voice rang out from the empty landing. 'I'm not in the room. Remember?'

'Sorry,' said Steel, as he wandered back up the stairs, still in thought. 'Sapphire?'

'Yes?'

'Can you try to take Time back?'

'I can try, yes.'

Steel had climbed to the highest, safe point on the stairs once more. 'Even ten minutes would do. But no less.'

'Alright. I'll try.'

'Rob?'

Helen had appeared at the foot of the stairs. She still wore her nightclothes and her eyes were heavy with sleep. Steel and Rob looked down the stairs at the small, tired figure.

'Go back to sleep, Helen,' Rob said, trying to copy Steel's manner of sharpness.

'No.' Helen began to climb the stairs. 'I want Sapphire. Where is she?'

Steel jabbed a finger in the direction of the hallway. 'Keep her down there,' he ordered.

Moving quickly down the stairs, Rob intercepted his sister. 'Is she upstairs?' Helen asked, refusing to budge from the second step.

'Quickly.' Steel was calling to the landing. 'Try taking it back now.'

'Alright.'

'I can hear her.' Helen looked around her at the sound of Sapphire's voice.

'Quickly. Now.'

'But I can't see her.' Helen stared up at Rob. 'Where is she?' She tugged at Rob's sleeve.

Rob, still watching the operation at the top of the stairs, reached down and held Helen's hand tightly. 'Please be quiet, Helen,' he murmured.

But Helen had decided to call out at the top of her voice. 'Where are you, Sapphire?'

Steel turned round quickly, angrily, as Rob placed his hand over Helen's mouth.

'I'm alright, Helen,' Sapphire's voice floated down from the landing. 'Just do as Rob says.'

Helen's eyes looked around the stairs and the hallway. Mystified, she nodded her head at thin air.

'I said quickly.' Steel was facing the landing again. 'There won't be time left. Take it back now!'

And, once again, there was an uneasy period of silence as Rob and Steel watched the landing. Yet Rob felt confident. He remembered the way that Sapphire had dealt with Constable Daly. It had been simple on her part. No effort at all. He could visualise the blueness of her eyes right now as she concentrated on, and dealt with, whatever it was that was threatening her, that was keeping her trapped in that strange, invisible room.

'Steel?'

Sapphire's voice surprised Rob slightly. He had unconsciously believed that the next logical step was Sapphire's reappearance. Not that isolated voice that seemed to speak from nowhere.

'Yes?' Steel's voice was just faintly apprehensive.

'It's not working, Steel.'

Helen shifted her head to look up at Rob. But Rob held on to her tightly and put one finger to his lips as he watched both the landing and Steel's face.

'What d'you mean, it's not working?'

'It isn't. I've tried, but nothing happens. It won't go back. It refuses to. Therefore *we* can't go back.'

'Try again,' Steel urged her. 'Quickly.'

They waited. Rob felt a tiny sensation. It was like a movement, he thought. Or rather, like an intended movement. As if he had meant to do something, meant to go somewhere, and then found that he had changed his mind without having made the effort to move.

'It's still no use, Steel.'

'Try! Keep trying!'

'Yes.'

Slowly, clearly, Sapphire's voice was beginning to lose its calmness.

Rob could feel the same slight sensation again. Like being in a lift that has stopped while someone is trying all sorts of knobs and switches to get the thing started again.

'No.' It was almost a shout of protest from Sapphire now. 'Please, Steel. It's no good. It's in here with me.'

'Sapphire . . .?'

'Can't you see it?'

They saw it. Helen was already pointing a finger at the landing as Rob looked. Steel had already noticed it.

The patch of light was shining palely through the picture, glowing through the grim structure of the cottage.

'Look!' cried Rob.

Steel stared at the patch of light. 'Yes,' he said, quietly. 'We can see it, Sapphire.'

'Good. Because it's fighting me. It's holding me here.' Sapphire's voice now sounded anxious. 'It's fighting me and it's winning.' Then quickly, 'Do you hear me, Steel?'

'Yes, Sapphire.' He turned from the landing. 'Just wait.'

'I haven't much choice, have I?'

But Steel, with a determined look on his face, was already walking down the stairs.

'What are you going to do?' Rob called after him.

'Deal with it.' Steel eased his way past Helen. When he had reached the hallway, Steel looked back. 'In the meantime, keep your sister where she is and keep Sapphire talking.'

'Right,' said Rob. And Steel walked quickly towards the kitchen without once looking back.

Rob stood there on the stairs for a moment. Then, still holding Helen's hand, he walked up the next two steps with her and stopped. Just two small figures looking up at an empty landing and the weird patch of light.

'Sapphire?' Rob called.

It seemed a moment or two before there was an answer. 'Yes?'

'Is it like the wall?'

'The what?'

'The wall in Helen's room. Is that— is that thing like it?'

There was another pause before Sapphire answered. 'It's a part of it. A fragment. So don't come near it. Don't come near the landing.'

'No.' Rob looked down at Helen who smiled back up at him,

76

anxiously. Rob cleared his throat and faced the landing once more. 'I'm supposed to keep you talking,' he announced.

'You're doing fine,' was the wry reply.

'Sapphire?' Helen could not locate the source of the voice but she had decided to call out anyway, peering in various directions as she did so.

'Hallo, Helen.'

'I want to see you, Sapphire.'

There was yet another long moment of silence.

'Soon, Helen. Soon.' Sapphire's voice seemed to swallow slightly on the words. 'You just be patient, will you?'

'Yes.' Helen nodded at the empty air around her.

Both children failed to notice the tiny increase of power from the patch of light. Just a faint, momentary brightening of the pale glow.

On the attic landing, around the edges of the boarded-up room, there was a sudden, luminous flicker, as if in answer to the one below. Then two more patches of light eased themselves out from under the darkness of the door. Accompanied by the mini-rumbling sound, the two patches of light glided across the landing floor. At the top of the cupboard-stair they stopped and waited.

Behind the door, in the attic bedroom, the low, whispered voice continued with its endless chanting. *'Upstairs and downstairs, Upstairs and downstairs . . .'*

The two Ironside troopers appeared on the stairs. Like the voice, their intentions seemed, at first, to be as repetitive and as mechanical as before. Then, as the troopers, with drawn swords, reached the landing, the two patches of light moved forward to meet them. The lights seemed to blend in with the bodies of the troopers. As they did so, their sounds and the glow faded.

And this time the troopers stopped before they reached the attic room door. Both figures turned, moved back across the landing and began to descend the stairs.

Behind the door, the quiet voice kept up its variation.

'I'll tell you one thing, Rob.' Sapphire's voice spoke out to the two children still waiting on the stairs.

'What's that?' Rob asked.

'I'm glad of the rhyme that you chose. You might have settled for "Oranges and Lemons".'

Rob thought about it for a second or two and then realised as he remembered Sapphire's description of the block and the axe.

He glanced towards the picture. The glow of light was still visible.

Sapphire's voice sounded a little edgy as her words tumbled from her once more. 'Then again, if Roundhead soldiers belong anywhere, I suppose they belong in this hell-hole of a room.'

Rob was about to adopt Steel's instructions and warn Sapphire not to think about the cottage room, when her voice suddenly shouted at him.

'Rob! Do you hear that?'

Rob listened. He could hear nothing.

'Hear what?'

'Footsteps. Heavy footsteps. On stone— on stone steps. Can you hear them, Rob?'

There was still nothing to be heard, but Rob felt his sister hold his hand tightly, squeezing it, and he, too, felt scared.

'They're coming here, Rob.' Sapphire's voice was louder still now. 'Climbing down stone steps. Coming to this room. They're going to smash the door of this room.'

'Sapphire . . .'

But Sapphire's voice cried out. 'Something happened here! Something terrible!'

Rob and Helen stared at the finely carved table and the careful arrangement of dried flowers that decorated the peaceful-looking first-floor landing.

'Rob!' It was almost a scream now. 'Get Steel! Quickly!'

But Rob was already running down the last few steps to the hallway.

'Please! Help me!' Sapphire's voice seemed to fill the deserted landing area.

But there was only the small frightened figure of Helen watching from the staircase.

Chapter Ten

Rob was shoving open the kitchen door as Steel crossed the room from the direction of the empty office. 'Steel...' Rob began. And then he stopped.

Walking at medium pace and looking almost mechanical, Steel was approaching Rob and the open kitchen door. Steel's face was ash white and his stare was fixed firmly on the doorway and the hallway beyond.

'Don't come near me.' Steel said as he walked. 'Don't speak to me. Don't touch me.'

The voice, too, sounded unhuman. Rob moved back from the doorway, allowing Steel to pass. As he did so, Rob felt a blast of icy coldness. It was coming from Steel. It was like opening the door of a cold storage plant. Rob moved away quickly. 'But you're cold— you're freezing.'

'I said, don't come near me.' Steel cautioned him, as he moved through the doorway and into the hall. Once there, Steel kept on walking, straight towards the first staircase, with Rob following after him at a safe, warm distance.

Helen turned to stare, wide-eyed, as Steel began to climb the stairs.

'Keep the child away from me.'

Rob scrambled up the first two or three steps, keeping behind, and to one side, of Steel. Rob reached forward and grabbed Helen's arm, pulling her clear of Steel's path.

'Quickly! Please!' Sapphire's hollow voice was still shouting.

Steel walked slowly and steadily up the stairs, as if he had no intention of stopping before he reached the landing.

Sapphire's voice continued to call out. 'Somebody died in this room. A young girl.'

Rob looked quickly at the picture. The glow of light was still there.

'And it wants me to be her, wants it to happen all over again,' said Sapphire's unseen voice.

'No, Sapphire,' Helen cried out, frightened. And Rob held her tightly as Steel carried on climbing the stairs. He had almost reached the top.

'And the girl's killers are here. Outside. They're breaking down the door, Steel.'

Steel reached the landing. He did not stop walking. For a brief second, Rob remembered the warning about what would happen to anyone who stepped on to the landing. But some instinct told him that this ice-cold, white-faced Steel did not happen to be just anyone at this moment.

Steel walked on to the landing without stopping. Rob saw him walk straight to the picture, reaching up and out with his hands as he did so. He then touched the picture with the flat of both hands.

Rob and Helen stared. They saw the picture, and the surrounding area of wall, instantly cloud up and frost over. There was an odd cry. It was similar to the fabric sound, but this was more like a shrill cry of pain, the kind that a small animal might make. The patch of light appeared to glow brighter and then was still, as if frozen there. It then tipped and fell from the picture. It seemed to spin, like a lit shuttlecock, down the wall and on to the floor as Sapphire reappeared on the landing.

'Sapphire!' Rob found himself crying out with relief as he saw her. And Helen, too, was trying to rush forward to greet Sapphire.

But Rob had seen the troopers.

'There!' Rob shouted a warning as he ran up the stairs towards the landing.

The two troopers had appeared from the second flight of stairs. They were moving across the landing, moving towards the turned backs of Sapphire and Steel.

6

But Steel was aware of them. He swung around quickly to face them. And Rob, running on to the landing, wondered why he had bothered to shout out. After all, these ghosts, or whatever they were, couldn't hurt you. That had already been proved.

This time, though, the troopers did not pass through the air like ghosts. The first one walked right into Rob. Rob heard the jingle of metal and could smell leather and the musty odour of decay as he felt the full force of the impact. He was thrown backwards, pitching and stumbling, the sword missing his head as it was swung across and down.

'It's in them, Steel.'

Rob heard Sapphire's cry as he hit the landing floor and rolled over.

'The light's in them. Carried through. The girl died . . .' Sapphire stopped talking as the second trooper grabbed her.

Rob saw it all as he rolled over and looked up. He saw Sapphire thrown back against the wall, under the picture. He saw the trooper reaching with his free hand, reaching and dragging down an invisible length of rope. The first trooper had turned. He was looking down at Rob. And Rob could see the ancient, skull-like face under the helmet visor. He thought that he could hear himself screaming, and then realised, through the fear and the confusion, that it was Helen's voice that cried out in fear.

The first trooper was raising the sword again. From where Rob lay, it seemed to be a mile high, but still above him. And then he saw Steel moving, his hands reaching out, palms extended. Steel touched both troopers simultaneously. The cloud-like, freezing frost appeared in the air and upon the troopers, like white mist. There was the shrill cry of pain once more, the shifting movement of light, and then the troopers disappeared.

As Rob dragged himself to his feet he saw two patches of light moving swiftly, climbing the second flight of stairs. Their strange sound rustled an accompaniment as they retreated to the darkness and safety of the landing above.

By the time Rob had turned to see why Steel was not giving

chase, the two patches of light moved out of sight. But, at that moment, Rob no longer cared. He was more concerned about Steel.

Leaning back against the opposite wall, Steel looked tired and ill. He was breathing deeply, as if all his energy had been drained from him.

Sapphire had been comforting Helen. But now she released the child as she moved to the sick-looking Steel.

'He said not to touch him,' Rob remembered.

'It's alright now,' said Sapphire, as she took Steel's hands and began to massage some circulation back into them.

'Not enough. We didn't do enough.' Steel murmured, his eyes half closed.

'Yes we did.' Sapphire eased Steel's fingers to and fro.

Steel shook his head weakly. 'Not enough to stop them. Not enough to hold them.'

'But we've held that one.' Sapphire indicated with a nod of her head. 'Look.'

The first patch of light was on the floor, directly beneath the picture. It still appeared to be in a frozen state. It was like the spot at the end of a beam of light, but without the beam. Also, unlike normal light, it was not transparent. The pattern of the rug, on which it lay, could not be seen through it.

'Oh, yes,' said Steel. Then he closed his eyes and rested his head back against the wall.

'What's wrong with him?' asked Rob.

'Go down into the kitchen, will you?' said Sapphire. 'Make up the fire.' She put her arms around Steel and helped him away from the wall. 'And make sure it's a good fire.'

'Yes,' said Rob and began to hurry down the stairs.

'Come on, Steel.' Sapphire put her arm about Steel's waist to support him. 'We need you well again,' she said as she helped him towards the top of the stairs, then added, 'As soon as possible.'

Helen moved to help Sapphire. And Rob, looking up from the hallway, felt a sadness and a fear as he watched the tall figure of Sapphire, and the small shape of Helen assisting Steel as he moved feebly down the stairs.

'That fire.' Sapphire reminded him.

'Sorry,' said Rob and hurried along the hallway to the kitchen.

The stove in the kitchen was blazing brightly. The big parlour chair had been pulled up to the fire and Steel was sat in it. Although his eyes were still closed and he seemed asleep, some of the colour had returned to his face. Helen's blanket was draped about his shoulders.

Helen sat on a stool by the fire and watched Steel as Sapphire stacked provisions, that had earlier been in the freezer, into the refrigerator.

It was what happened to his mother's freezer that had, at first, concerned Rob. The heavy cabinet, minus its lid, was now in the cleared-out office, and a make-shift dial had been attached to the freezer motor. The freezer lid was set against a wall near the door.

Rob stood in the lobby, looking in at the office. The room was much colder now. In fact, even the freezer seemed colder than normal. The iced frost effect, that had helped to get rid of the troopers, could be seen all along the panelling that housed the machine's power source.

And it had all been done by Steel in a very short space of time. It was there, like this, when they had brought Steel, semi-conscious, down from the landing. A large, heavy sheet of bevelled glass, that had once been the top of Rob's father's favourite table, was now leaning against the far office wall. All Steel's handiwork. Except that there was one extra item in the office now. If it could be called an item. The thing that was imprisoned in the freezer cabinet.

Rob wandered back into the kitchen. Sapphire was closing the refrigerator door. She looked up as Rob crossed the room to look at Steel.

'Is he better yet?' Rob asked.

'Not yet, no,' said Sapphire. 'But he will be.'

'Fire.' Steel murmured, his eyes still closed.

Sapphire moved quickly across the room to the fireside.

'Has the fire gone out?' Steel shivered slightly.

'No.' Sapphire gathered the blanket around him. 'It's still burning. Still hot.'

Steel seemed to relax. 'Oh,' he muttered, and began to doze again.

Sapphire picked up the poker and stirred the coals of the stove.

Rob looked at the sleeping Steel, then asked, 'What did he do?'

'Do?' asked Sapphire, innocently.

'Before he came up the stairs. Before he rescued you. He must have done something. He was like ice. I couldn't stand near him.'

Sapphire replaced the poker. 'Yes, he did do something.' And there was the slight smile in her eyes, the joke. 'He took himself down.'

Rob stared at her. 'Down?'

Sapphire nodded. 'To about minus two-seven-three degrees, I think it is, in your temperature scale.'

Rob was still looking at her in astonishment when she asked, 'Well, it did the trick, didn't it?'

'So if I'd touched him . . .?'

'You would have been instantly drained of heat.' Sapphire pointed towards the office. 'Like that thing in there.'

Turning his head to look towards the office, Rob felt grateful for Steel's warning.

'The— the piece of light.' Steel murmured once more, eyes closed.

'I'm dealing with it,' said Sapphire.

'You've followed my instructions?'

'Yes.'

'Because it— it must be kept— same temperature.'

'I know that.'

'Mustn't regain— mustn't regain its heat.' And Steel's words had become more slurred as he settled his head back on the chair and slept once more.

Sapphire moved back to Steel's side. She touched at his face and forehead, testing for warmth.

'It takes all his strength away then, does it?' asked Rob, intrigued by Steel's condition and the reason for it. 'Going down to that temperature and back.'

'Yes,' said Sapphire.

'So there's only us, then?' Helen's small voice spoke up at last.

Sapphire and Rob looked at her.

'If the thing comes back,' Helen added.

Rob looked at his sister. He then glanced towards the hallway door, then back to Sapphire.

Yet again, Sapphire had read his thoughts. 'We'll be alright,' she said, but her assurance did not sound completely convincing.

Steel stirred again, loosening his blanket, and Sapphire reached out to him.

'Just rest now,' she whispered. 'Sleep.' And she tucked the blanket firmly around Steel's tired shoulders. 'And you two,' she said, looking at Rob and Helen. 'You must get some sleep.'

Although he felt tired, sleep was the last thing Rob wanted at this moment. Not that he was really scared to go to bed on his own, he told himself. There was Sapphire to consider. Now that Steel was temporarily out of action, someone had to help her, was his excuse to himself.

'I'm not tired,' he announced.

'And I've been asleep.' Helen threw in for good measure.

Sapphire looked at the two of them for a moment. 'Alright, then,' she said. 'You'd better help me until you do feel sleepy.' And she turned and walked towards the office.

Sapphire had been doing some adjusting with the freezer's make-shift dial, and now the bare room seemed even colder still.

Rob and Helen felt the cold as they stood in the office and watched Sapphire. They had pulled their gowns tightly around them and they had folded their arms to keep the warmth in.

The only sound was the steady hum of the freezer cabinet's motor.

'Look, Rob.' Helen had shuffled forward and was now peering, on tip-toe, into the open cabinet.

Rob glanced at Sapphire, but she seemed unconcerned as she set the dial, so Rob wandered to the cabinet and peered in over Helen's shoulder.

The patch of light was at the bottom of the otherwise empty cabinet. It seemed to be huddled up in one corner. Against the white surfaces of the cabinet's interior, and the film of glistening frost, the patch of light seemed much paler, almost difficult to see at first glance. To Rob, it was like something, some unknown threat, floating just below the surface of the sea, on a hot, bright day.

'Steel said that it was—well, that it was just a fragment.' Rob shivered as he stared into the open cabinet.

'It is,' said Sapphire, reaching for the sheet of heavy glass. 'Help me with this, will you?'

As well as being thick, the sheet of glass was long. As long and a little wider than the cabinet.

'A fragment of what's in the top room?' asked Rob, as he and Helen moved to the sheet of glass.

Sapphire nodded. Then, with the help of Rob and Helen, she eased the sheet of heavy glass away from the wall. The three of them struggled but managed to lift the glass over the top of the freezer cabinet. The glass made a dull, ringing sound as it was lowered on to the cabinet.

Rob breathed out from the effort as Helen stood on her toes once more, to peer through the sheet of heavy glass.

'Is it alive?' she asked as she looked at the captive patch of light.

Sapphire nodded again. 'Yes.'

'Is it hurt?'

'Who cares if it's hurt?' Rob snapped at his sister. 'It tried to kill Sapphire. Remember?'

'Oh, yes.' Fascinated by the object in the cabinet, Helen had temporarily forgotten just how dangerous that patch of light could be.

Sapphire was also looking at the glass as it began to frost over from the inside, forming a canopy of ice.

'More like children,' Sapphire said, thoughtfully.

Rob looked at her. 'Children?'

'Alright then, offspring. Living additions. Growing successors.' She left Rob to take his pick as she moved away from the cabinet.

Rob stared at the white-misted glass. 'Is it something that you've seen before?' he wanted to know.

Sapphire stood in the centre of the bleak office room and looked back at the cabinet. 'Not quite.'

'As dangerous as anything you've seen before?'

Sapphire remained in thought for a moment or two before answering, 'More dangerous.'

Rob and Helen turned slowly to look at Sapphire.

'But there's two more of those things somewhere in the house.' Rob exclaimed.

'I know,' said Sapphire. Then, as if to change the subject, 'Come on, back in the warm.'

And she walked to the door, the two children following her. Sapphire pointed at the detached freezer lid as she passed it. 'You can put that on the cellar steps for me before you go to bed.'

Rob and Helen had half-carried, half-dragged the freezer lid through the kitchen, into the hallway and on to the cellar steps. It had been hard work, but at least the effort had made them warm. Rob had asked Sapphire, while she was directing them through the kitchen, why Steel could not do, to the attic room wall, what he had done to the patches of light. 'That would only suspend it for a while,' she had answered, explaining that even Steel's talents could not stop Time for always. 'That would be like trying to freeze the universe with one cube of ice,' was her final comment and she had returned to stoke up the fire for Steel's benefit, leaving Rob and Helen to struggle out into the hallway with the freezer lid.

'But if it's a child...' Helen said as Rob closed the cellar door on the heavy lid.

'Who said it's a child?' Rob flexed his tired muscles,

yawning as he did so. He felt weary, and the last thing he wanted now was one of Helen's entangling conversations.

'Sapphire did. She said so. So, if the thing we caught is a child . . .'

'Sapphire didn't say that. Well she didn't mean it that way.'

'Oh.'

'She said children first. Then she said offspring. That means pups or cubs . . .'

'Its young.'

'What?' Rob looked at his sister, impatiently.

'At school they call it its young.'

'Do they?' said Rob, without interest, as he checked to see if the cellar door was properly closed. He then began to move back towards the comfort of the kitchen, while Helen pattered along behind him on slippered feet.

'So what if its parents come looking for it?' Helen asked.

Rob stopped walking. As usual, Helen had scored with one of her random remarks. He turned slowly to look at Helen.

'Steel could handle it,' he said.

'But he's not well.'

Rob glanced towards the dark staircase, then back. He was about to tell Helen that Steel would probably not be out of action for very long, and, until then, he and Sapphire could cope, when there was a loud knocking on the entrance door.

Startled, Rob and Helen turned to look at the door. There had been no sound of approach from outside. No car. No footsteps. No kind of warning whatsoever.

'Who is it, Rob?' Helen whispered.

'How do I know?'

'Perhaps it's the policeman.'

Rob stood there. Apart from not being able to cope at this precise moment, he also found it difficult to think, to even move.

The knocking came again. It was not sharp. It was more like a dull booming sound. As if a heavy fist was being used by whoever was out there.

Noticing Rob's statue-like stance, Helen decided to deal with things. 'I'll see,' she said, walking to the door.

Rob moved at last. 'Helen!'

He moved after his sister and stopped her as she reached the door.

'But we have to answer it, Rob.'

Rob looked at Helen, then at the door. His first thought, at this moment, was to shout for Sapphire. But, as man of the house now, theoretically, he ought to be showing some initiative. Especially with his sister watching. Anyway, it was their house, their front door. And, at the present time, anyone on the outside could hardly be more than a threat than something from the inside, from upstairs say. So these were his thoughts of action as he stood there rooted to the floor once again.

'Rob!' Helen was already crouching down to draw back the bottom bolt of the door.

'Alright.' Rob made the decision. He reached up and drew back the top bolt. He reached for the catch.

The door was pushed open, violently, as if whoever was out there had lost patience. Small pieces of splintered wood and screws were scattered as the catch was forced from the door, which swung open with a great deal of force, shuddering and bouncing as it hit the door-stop.

Rob and Helen, on instinct, had moved quickly away from the door at the first sound of impact. They looked back— and up.

A man was in the doorway. He seemed to fill the doorway completely, so that nothing could be seen of the outside. If Sapphire could be described as light, bright blue, then this huge man was dark blue. Like ink. Even his clothes, which looked like the clothes of a merchant seaman, were dull blue or navy coloured.

He looked down at Rob and Helen, an impassive expression on his large face. Like the kind of calmness that often preceded an explosion.

Rob and Helen could only have looked up at the towering figure for a fraction of a second before they started running towards the safety of the kitchen.

Chapter Eleven

'A giant?' asked Sapphire.

'Yes,' said Helen.

'No, a man, but— well, he is.' Rob agreed. 'He's almost a giant.'

Sapphire looked towards the door. Keeping close to her, the two children also looked, and listened.

There was no sound from outside in the hallway.

Steel was still asleep in the chair. He had been like that when Rob and Helen had first run into the kitchen with their news. Sapphire had been in the office, but she came out quickly when they had called to her.

Now, as they regained their breath, Rob and Helen waited for Sapphire to think of something.

'In the front doorway, you say?' Sapphire was still looking towards the hallway door.

'Yes,' said Rob.

'He appeared there?'

'No. He knocked on the door.'

'Then I— well, Helen and I— tried to open the door. But he pushed it open, broke the lock.'

'He came from outside?' Sapphire asked as she walked slowly towards the hallway door, Rob and Helen close at her heels.

'Yes,' said Rob. 'Not from inside the house.'

Sapphire halted by the door which was, as Rob and Helen had left it, just slightly ajar.

'So he wasn't one of the soldiers?'

'No,' said Rob. 'He was dressed in ordinary clothes. Anyway, he was bigger than the soldiers.'

'He's a giant, Sapphire,' whispered Helen, moving close to her.

Sapphire put her arm around Helen. 'Alright, alright,' she said, calming the child. Sapphire glanced at Steel, who was still asleep, she then angled her head to listen at the partly open door. There was no sound from the hallway.

Withdrawing her head, Sapphire spoke quietly. 'Did he enter the house?'

Rob shrugged. 'I don't know. We didn't wait to see.'

Sapphire nodded, then reached out carefully for the door handle.

'Can't we wake Steel?' asked Rob, quickly.

'No.' Sapphire began to ease the door gently open. 'I'm afraid, for the time being, it's just the three of us.'

She looked out into the hallway, and Rob and Helen peered out with her.

The hallway was deserted. The front door was closed. Rob noticed this. He was about to whisper the fact to Sapphire when she nodded, having read his thought yet again.

'Now follow me. But be very quiet and do as I say.' Sapphire whispered the instructions quietly. 'Understand?'

Rob and Helen both nodded.

Sapphire led them both through the doorway and into the hall, one on either side of her, a hand on each of their shoulders. They moved, like a small formation, along the quiet hallway.

Rob was beginning to think, even hope, that it was another trick. Another illusion projected by whatever was in the room upstairs. The entrance door was closed, so maybe the lock was still intact. Perhaps the door had not really been forced open after all. Visual refractions, Sapphire had called the soldiers, before the light had got into them. Well, perhaps the big man was the same. And visual refractions could not break real doors. They could make you think it . . .

'Look!' said Helen as they reached the door.

Rob looked. The door was closed, but the lock was still broken. Screws and pieces of splintered wood lay on the floor around the door. The bolts were still drawn back.

Looking up at Sapphire, Rob wished that she would take

them all back to the kitchen immediately. Once there, they could always barricade the door and wait for Steel to recover. Maybe even force him to recover.

But Sapphire was reaching out for the iron handle of the door. She jerked the door open and swung it back as far as it would go.

There was no-one in the doorway and no-one outside the door.

'Hallo, Sapphire.'

The deep, resonant voice came from inside the house. Sapphire, Rob and Helen all turned to look.

The big man, in the dark clothes, was sitting on a step halfway up the first staircase. He seemed to cover the width of the stair.

'Anything to eat in this place?' said the man. 'I'm starving.'

'It's him,' whispered Helen as she tugged at Sapphire's dress. 'It's the giant.'

Sapphire looked at the man for a moment, then turned and closed the door. 'Yes, I suppose you could call him that,' she said, quite calmly, as she pushed home the top bolt. 'But his name's Lead.'

'Lead?' said Rob, bewildered.

Sapphire nodded. 'That's right. Lead.'

The man stretched his arms, flexed his shoulders, then eased his large frame into a standing position. 'So where is he?' his voice boomed. 'Where's Steel?'

Steel's eyes opened slowly. He looked up. Lead's tall shape threw a long shadow over Steel and the chair and the area around the fireplace.

'Lead?' Steel murmured, tilting his head back to look up. 'Is that Lead? Here?'

'Yes.' The big man nodded patiently, almost wearily. 'I'm here.'

When Sapphire had taken Lead into the kitchen, Steel had been still asleep in the chair by the fire. But he had seemed more relaxed in sleep. His breathing was regular and his body no longer shuddered feverishly at the cold inside it.

Sapphire had given Lead some food, and Rob and Helen had sat at the table and watched the man as he ate. A half a loaf of bread, held in his massive hand, looked like a sandwich at a village fete, Rob thought.

But, apart from his size, his obvious strength and his world-weary smile, Lead was pleasant enough. In fact, compared to Steel he was positively friendly. And Rob had thought about the name, Lead. It suited the man in the same physical way that made the names Sapphire and Steel seem so appropriate. Rob was reminded of the protective flashings and the lead-covered areas of roof on the old house. The dark, heavy, bluish metal that was like a kind of armour.

Sapphire had explained what had happened in the house, and Lead had listened and nodded as he ate his meal. When Lead had asked if anyone in the house had been taken, Sapphire had glanced at Rob before telling Lead about the disappearance of Rob's parents. She had said it as tactfully as possible, but Rob had felt the cramped feeling of sadness inside him, like a quick dull pain.

The big man, Lead, seemed to have noticed. He had looked up from his food and gazed directly at Rob. 'It's alright, son,' the man had said, his deep voice rumbling out the words. 'They'll get your parents back for you— somehow.' And he had returned to his meal, and Sapphire had moved to the stove, picked up the scuttle and shaken more fuel on to the hot coals.

'I mean, you can guarantee it, can't you?' Lead was looking down at the blanket-covered Steel. 'You can guarantee I'm here. Whenever you decide to wander off and ice yourself up, without me around, you're in trouble.'

Rob looked at Sapphire and noticed that she smiled slightly at this. But the bantering seemed to work. It started a spark, began to bring Steel back to his old self.

'I am *not* in trouble.' Steel said, shaking the blanket from his shoulders.

Lead seemed unimpressed. 'Alright, then.' He ambled back

towards the kitchen table. 'You're not in trouble. You don't need help . . .'

'No . . .'

'But you need insulation.'

Steel moved forward in the chair as Lead continued, 'And that's me.' He tapped his broad chest and sat himself down at the table once more, making Rob wonder if the man was ready to eat again now that a good half an hour had passed since the meal.

'You tell him, Sapphire.' Lead waved his hand as if to dismiss Steel, as if he had better things to do than pick up the pieces for others. 'You tell him he shouldn't be doing that below zero stuff without me around to protect him.'

Sapphire said nothing. She did not have to. Again it worked. Steel flung the blanket down and stood up from the chair. He turned to face the others.

Rob felt better as he climbed into the make-shift bed in the sitting room. Helen had fallen asleep the moment she had snuggled under the blankets on the couch. Sapphire tucked the blankets in around her, then moved back to the door, opened it and switched off the central light.

'Are there many others?' asked Rob, sitting up in the bed.

'Others?' Sapphire stood in the dark doorway of the room.

'Others like you. And Steel. And Lead.'

Sapphire considered the question for a moment or two. 'About a hundred and twenty-seven,' she said eventually, and then gave the tease of a smile as she added, 'Not counting the non-basic elements.'

Before Rob could ask another question, Sapphire put her finger to her lips.

'Go to sleep now. We've a lot to do tomorrow.'

Sapphire then pulled the door to and left Rob to lie in the bed and think. And he felt more secure down here on the ground floor, with a small table-lamp to counteract the dark, and knowing that Sapphire, Steel and Lead were all close at hand in the kitchen.

And he felt more confident now. Steel had recovered, Sapphire was in her usual fine form, and Lead had arrived to help them. And he wondered how the thing in the attic room would be reacting at this moment, now that they were at full strength with even a captive to bargain with, if they wanted to bargain. Perhaps, under the circumstances, the thing would ask for its 'child' back.

Then Mum and Dad could be returned and everything could be peaceful once more.

Calmed by these thoughts, Rob fell asleep. He slept soundly.

From behind the nailed-up door, on the attic landing, there was a single flicker of light. Then there was darkness again for a long time before the light pulsated once more from inside the room. It was like a signal.

Down in the darkness of the cold office room there was a similar glimmer of light. It came from inside the converted cabinet. A single dull flash that glowed and made patterns through the iced-up sheet of heavy glass.

And, on the attic landing, the light behind the door replied in turn. The glow was then extinguished, as if whatever was behind the door had received an answer and was satisfied.

Chapter Twelve

The painting that had trapped Sapphire was the first to be taken down. It was Rob's job to remove every picture while Helen helped Sapphire to collect up all the books.

One picture in particular was extra heavy. It had also been hung in an awkward place, halfway up the second staircase. Rob was trying to ease the cumbersome picture from the wall as Lead appeared from below and began to climb the stairs. He raised his arm as Helen squeezed by him with half a dozen books.

'Where's Steel?' Lead asked.

'Top landing,' said Rob, still struggling with the large picture.

Lead nodded and moved on up the stairs. As he passed Rob, he reached out and plucked the heavily framed picture from the wall with finger and thumb, as if it were a sheet of paper. He did this in one action, without stopping, lowering the picture down on to the stair as he passed by.

'Given you all the rough jobs, has he?' Lead grinned as he moved on up the stairs, leaving Rob to marvel at the simple feat of strength.

The picture of the cottage had been burned, by Sapphire, in the kitchen stove, and its frame and glass stacked in the cellar. Since early that morning, another fifteen pictures had suffered a similar fate. So, too, had most of the books. At first, Rob had been concerned about how his parents would have felt about some of their most cherished possessions being destroyed. Then it had dawned on him that those very possessions had been instrumental in the disappearance of his parents. Each

7.

one of those treasured objects, a potential trigger. The rare old sea prints, the framed eighteenth-century maps, the few first editions, even the small book of sonnets, that his father had bought as a love token for his mother during their courting days, were possible traps.

Sapphire had said that the burning of the books and the paintings was an emergency measure. A precaution. Looking at the large picture that Lead had removed from the wall, Rob was inclined to agree with her. The picture was of an old sailing ship that had been wrecked in a storm. The artist had painted dark, ominous clouds, wreckage and sailors drowning in a wild looking sea. 'What if a patch of light had got into this picture,' Rob thought, and wondered how long Sapphire would have survived, had that one been chosen instead of the cottage.

Deciding to get the thought out of his mind, Rob tried picking the picture up with his finger and thumb, then with one hand. Neither way could he lift it. He tilted the picture on to its back, then began to slide it down the stairs to the landing below.

In the kitchen, flames burned from the stove. The hob lid was off and prints, pictures and books were stacked and waiting on the hearth. Sapphire was tearing up a picture. She dropped the pieces into the flames as Helen entered with the half dozen books.

'Thank you,' said Sapphire, as Helen placed the books down on the hearth, then walked back to the door.

'Spare room next?' asked Helen.

Sapphire nodded. 'Spare room next.'

As Helen left the room, Sapphire put the last piece of the picture in the fire. She then reached out for yet another one.

Rob had dragged the heavy picture down to the hallway and left it there with the others that were due to have their glass and frames removed.

Having now cleared the first two staircases and landings,

Rob climbed back up to the second landing and opened the cupboard-stair door. He then began taking down the small set of prints that were hung on the narrow walls.

He listened as he heard the voices of Steel and Lead talking on the landing above.

'You want to take yourself down and walk in *there*?' Lead was saying.

'Yes,' was Steel's answer.

'Walk into *that*?'

Interested, Rob climbed the stairs and peered between the bannisters to look and listen.

Steel and Lead were standing and studying the boarded-up door of the attic room.

'I'd like to be able to freeze it back,' Steel said, testing the wooden boards with his hands. 'At least as far as the wall.'

Lead pulled a face. He lowered his head and put his ear to the door to listen.

The mechanical voice beyond the door was still chanting, *'Upstairs and downstairs, Upstairs and downstairs, Upstairs and . . .'*

Lead turned away from the door, a doubtful look on his face. 'That's one hell of a chance for you to take,' was his comment.

'For *us* to take,' said Steel, coolly. Then, seeing the look on Lead's face, he added, 'You'll be in there with me. My insulation, remember?'

'Yes, I remember,' Lead gave a slight sigh, but he seemed, to Rob, to be quite resigned and philosophical about the proposed task, as if it was something to be expected when working with Steel.

'So when do you plan to do it?'

'*If* we do it, we'll go in there as soon as all the books and pictures have been destroyed.' Steel stared at the door for a moment or two. 'We can't afford to leave it any escape routes.'

Lead nodded and shrugged again. 'Ah, well,' he said as he turned towards the stairs, 'I suppose it can't be any worse than following you around on that flea-bitten, god-forsaken ship.'

And Lead grinned as he saw Rob's face at the bannisters. Steel, noticing the grin, turned to look.

'I thought you were supposed to be collecting pictures?'

'I am.' Rob replied.

'Then collect them,' said Steel, causing Lead to grin even more.

'He's back to normal,' thought Rob as he climbed back down the stairs and reached out for the nearest print. He then looked up to see that Lead was still looking at him, amused.

'Did you help on the ship, too?' asked Rob. Ever since Sapphire had told him, the thought of Time breaking through on a ship had fascinated him.

'Yeh, I did a day on it.' Lead had obviously not been that impressed with the job at sea.

'What was the name of the ship?'

'I don't know.' Lead shook his head. 'What was it, Steel?'

'I forget,' said Steel.

'Blue something, wasn't it?'

'I said, I forget.'

Lead thought about it. 'Or was it Mary? Blue Mary? he asked himself, then shook his head again. 'No.'

And words and names from so many lessons at school raced through Rob's head. Mary, Maria, Marie, Blue, light blue, dark blue, sky blue— sky blue? He realised as the words formed silently on his mouth.

'Not the "Marie Celeste"?' he said excitedly, like someone who had made a momentous discovery.

Lead thought about it. 'Yeh, that's the one,' he said, unenthusiastically.

Helen had found eight books in the spare bedroom on the first floor. They were not large books, so she had no difficulty in carrying them to the door and out on to the landing.

As she approached the top of the stairs, she dropped one of the books. Clutching the remaining seven, she managed to reach down and retrieve the book. She tucked it back in with the others and began to descend the stairs.

Halfway down the stairs, the same book fell from her arms a second time.

The book hit the carpeted stairs, bounced down two or three steps and rested there, face upwards. It was the kind of book that might have appealed to Helen, had it been fairly new, with brightly coloured pictures. But this book was quite old and dull-looking. Its few illustrations were small, bleak pen-and-ink drawings. It was the kind of book that a grandmother or a great aunt might have possessed as a child. The title of the book, picked out in faded gold on the upturned cover, was 'Miscellaneous Rhymes and Fables'.

Helen clicked her tongue, moved down the stairs after the book and picked it up once again. She sat down on the stairs for a moment to adjust the batch of books in her arms, so that they could be held firmly and carried easily. Helen then descended the stairs to the hallway below without further difficulty, until she dropped the book for the third time.

It happened as she was entering the kitchen. If she had been a few years older, and had the alarmist imagination of a ten year old, she might have sworn that she did not drop the book but that it jumped from her, almost as if it did not want to enter the kitchen.

Sapphire was still burning pictures and books at the stove. 'Having trouble?' she asked, without turning from her work.

'Yes.' Helen picked up the book for what, to her, seemed the umpteenth time. She then carried the books across the kitchen and set them down by the stove, making sure that this particular book was on the top of the stack.

Sapphire poked at the fire and put out her hand for another book to burn, and Helen reached for the volume of rhymes and fables.

It was no longer on top of the others. It was lying, on its own, a good three feet away from the stove. Helen stared at it.

'Another one, please.' Sapphire was still waiting.

Handing Sapphire a small collection of magazines, Helen turned to the book of rhymes and fables once more. This time it had moved a further four feet away upon the floor, as if it was attempting, in stages, to move back towards the door, to get as far away from the stove as possible.

Helen made up her mind to waste no more time on the book.

She marched towards it, her hand reaching down for it.

The book opened itself, there on the floor.

With her hand still reaching out, Helen pulled up short, just in front of the book, the pages of which were flickering over and over, very fast, but not in a haphazard way, as if something unseen was looking through the book, looking for a certain page.

'Sapphire.' Helen called quietly, her eyes still watching the moving pages of the book.

Sapphire turned to look as Helen knelt down, fascinated, to peer at the turning pages.

'No, Helen.'

But even as Sapphire spoke and moved quickly across the room, the book stopped at an open page. And Helen was able to glimpse, before Sapphire pulled her away from the book, a page upon which was a short nursery-rhyme. Above the rhyme was a small illustration. A pen sketch of a song-bird, its feathers fluffed out, standing on an area of snow.

'But I know that rhyme, Sapphire,' Helen cried, as the word and the illustration seemed to jump from the page and project themselves in the very front of her mind.

'No!' Sapphire spoke sharply as she snatched up the book.

'But I do . . .'

'It *wants* you to know it.' Sapphire ripped the page from the book.

'It's in my head, Sapphire. It's in my head.'

The hob lid was still off and flames licked from the open stove as Sapphire hurried towards it with the page of rhyme. She crumpled the paper and dropped it into the fire.

The page of rhyme blew back out from the fire, straightening its crumpled shape as it rose in the air above the stove, as if it had no intention of being burned.

Sapphire grabbed at the page, but the piece of yellowed paper, with its rhyme and its sketch of a small bird, twisted and spiralled in the still air of the room, out of the reach of Sapphire's hands.

'Catch it, Helen! Catch it for me!'

The torn-out page pitched and swerved and swirled in the air, like a sail, like a kite gliding on a clear blustery day.

102

'I can't! I can't, Sapphire!' Helen put her small hands to the side of her head. 'I know it!'

'No!' Sapphire snatched wildly at the page and missed as it ducked within reach, then jerked away again.

'I do!' cried Helen. 'It's in my head! It won't go!'

Steel and Lead were descending the attic stairs when Steel stopped to look back.

Rob, at the foot of the stairs, had still been trying to learn more about the ship that appeared to have been the 'Marie Celeste', but neither Steel nor Lead had seemed concerned. He had tried telling them that it was an important mystery that people, clever people had been trying to solve for years, but even that had failed to stir their interest.

Rob had then argued that it could not have been the 'Marie Celeste' after all, because that ship had been found. Abandoned, but found. Whereas Steel had admitted sinking the ship.

'We sank the real one— yes,' Steel had said, before looking back up at the stairs.

'What's wrong, Steel? Lead asked, before Rob could ask any further questions.

Steel said nothing. Instead, he began to climb back up the attic stairs, fast. Lead and Rob followed behind him.

When he had reached the landing, Steel moved straight to the nailed-up door and scrutinised it. He knelt down, examining the gap at the bottom of the door as Lead and Rob watched him.

'Draw those curtains. Quickly.'

Lead moved to the small landing window and drew the short, but heavy curtains to shut out the daylight.

Steel continued to make a study of the attic bedroom door.

'What's wrong?' Lead asked again.

Steel rose slowly to his feet. He put his ear to the boards of the door and listened.

'The rhyme,' he said at last, turning to look at Lead, 'It's changed.'

The window in the kitchen burst open, its glass shattering across the room as the curtains fluttered and flapped inwards, and a biting cold wind, that was almost at gale force, blew into the room. The outside rear door broke its lock and crashed open. And the air was filled with dead leaves and debris that swept through the room and sucked up tablecloth and towels and papers and swung them around and around in the disturbed air.

Helen was blown to the ground, like a part of the debris. She put her arms about her head and screamed as Sapphire, the breath blown from her, ran and grabbed and snatched at the page. But the page dipped and dived and swung fast in the whirl and blast of the cold wind that blew crockery from the table and from the dresser shelves, smashing and bouncing the sharp, broken pieces across the floor. A work-box pitched from the top of the dresser, showering its contents as it fell to the floor. Helen, peering through covered eyes, saw pins cascade and reels of cotton bounce and spin across the floor, like tops on endless pieces of thread, while a pair of scissors plunged downwards, one of its blades thudding and sticking into the table-top, like a thrown knife.

Then the voice spoke. It was the same flat, mechanical voice that was once trapped in the attic room. But now it was no longer a whisper. It spoke above the storm that raged inside the kitchen.

> 'The north wind doth blow
> And we shall have snow . . .'

And Sapphire heard it as she scrambled and fought to catch the piece of paper on which was printed the rhyme and the small, innocent drawing of a song-bird.

> 'And what will poor Robin do then?
> Poor thing,'

In the office room, the ice on the converted freezer cabinet began to melt as the voice rang through the room.

'He'll sit in a barn . . .'

Steel, Lead and Rob watched as the light glowed from behind the attic room door.

'And keep himself warm . . .'

'Down the stairs!' Steel shouted to Rob, trying to match the power of the voice, which now seemed to fill every room and staircase in the house.

'And hide his head under his wing . . .'

The light flowed into the structure of the door and wooden bars, and spread itself out upon the landing.

'Poor thing.'

'It's coming out?' asked Lead, as he and Steel backed towards the stairs.

'Yes.'

'Coming through? Well, I can pull the roof down on it.' Lead reached up to seize the half-exposed support beam that spanned the attic ceiling.

'Won't work,' said Steel as the light grew brighter and the first, faint rumbling sound began.

And Rob, peering between the bannister rails, saw the wooden surface of the door, and its bars of wood, shift in the same way that the plaster of the attic room wall had shifted and formed another shape. As if they were melting, the jumbled shapes pressed forward once more, through the door and on to the landing. A parade of tumbling images, lit by the bright glow, the fabric sound rose to its inevitable, disturbing shriek, that would eventually penetrate the nerves and the brain.

Rob ran, stumbling down the stairs, as Steel and Lead moved after him.

'First a wall, then a room, then a house.' Rob remembered

Sapphire's warning as he tripped over, and smashed, the stacked prints in an effort to push open the cupboard-stair door. He glanced back to see that Lead was at the top of the stairs, moving backwards slowly, using his huge body, which was silhouetted against the glowing light, to protect Steel.

The cupboard-stair door opened and Rob staggered out on to the neat, orderly landing.

'Ro-ob!' he heard his mother's voice calling from the turmoil on the stairs. 'Wait for me, Rob.'

Rob did not want to hear it. He pressed his hands to his ears so that he could shut out the false, hurtful sound as Steel moved out on to the landing, followed by Lead.

'It's coming down after us.' Lead exclaimed as he slammed shut the cupboard-stair door, which immediately became filled with the glowing light, that seemed to pour itself into the door with a white hot molten effect that was brighter than the daylight.

In the wind-swept kitchen, the torn-out page continued to swerve and dive and twist in the air, as if in an attempt to dodge and torment the pursuing Sapphire.

Then it made one mistake as it dipped too low and skimmed across the surface of the table. Sapphire's hand moved quickly, snatching up the scissors that were embedded in the table-top, and jabbing downwards with them, in one quick movement. The scissor blade pierced the page, causing it to spin and twirl frantically, like a child's paper windmill, in an attempt to free itself. But Sapphire seized it and tore it from the scissor blade. Then, hurrying to the stove, she threw the ball of paper deep down on to the hot coals and slammed the hob lid into place.

The wind died instantly and there was quietness in the wrecked kitchen.

On the second landing, the sounds faded and the images receded. Steel, Lead and Rob watched as the glow became dimmer and the cupboard-stair door returned to normal.

Steel moved cautiously towards the door of the stair. He listened at it.

The mechanical voice was now whispering once more as it chanted its latest fragment of rhyme.

'Poor thing, Poor thing, Poor thing, Poor thing . . .'

Leaving Lead to guard the landing Steel began to descend the stairs. Rob followed him.

'It's alright now,' said Sapphire as she lifted the frightened Helen from the floor and held her close to her, comforting her. 'It's alright.'

Steel and Rob entered, and looked around them at the devastated room.

'A different rhyme,' said Sapphire.

'I know.' Steel moved to the outside door and slammed it shut, wedging it fast with a chair.

'It got into the child's head,' Sapphire explained, still holding the trembling Helen.

Steel walked to the broken window and closed it. 'And I said to watch her at all times.'

'It got into the book,' Sapphire insisted, 'A page in a book. Then into her head.'

Steel stared at Helen.

'It wasn't her fault then, was it?' said Rob, not happy with the hard, accusing way in which Steel stared at his sister.

Sapphire interrupted them, keeping the peace yet again. 'Anyway, I managed to burn the page, and the book,' she said as she walked Helen to the table, straightened a chair and sat the child down upon it.

Steel looked at the stove and the stacked-up books and paintings. He then turned and moved quickly across the room and into the office lobby.

'So where is it now?' Sapphire asked Rob.

'The attic landing and the attic stairs.'

'That far?' said Sapphire, and her face looked serious.

The freezer-cabinet had not completely defrosted, but it had been close. There was heavy condensation on the inside of the glass.

Steel tried to peer through the misty glass. He then felt the sides of the cabinet and seemed satisfied to find that it was still cold enough—just cold enough. He reached for the make-shift dial and set it to high.

He was watching the cabinet as the office door opened and Sapphire entered.

'It tried to melt it,' said Steel without turning, 'From a distance. It's capable of that.'

'When it has a rhyme,' said Sapphire, closing the door, 'It's capable of anything.' She moved to the cabinet and looked at it, watched the ice and frost re-forming on the inside of the glass. 'It wants its child back, I suppose.'

Steel said nothing as he waited for the cabinet to reach maximum coldness again.

'It gets nothing back from us,' he said. Then, as the dial needle reached its last mark, 'It's gained too much already.'

Steel then set the dial down and moved to the office door. He went out from the room and Sapphire followed him, closing the door to after her.

If the freezer cabinet had been completely defrosted, then Steel would have perhaps moved the sheet of glass, with its curtain of condensation, and looked inside the cabinet.

He would then have found that the cabinet was empty.

As if it had waited, just long enough for Sapphire and Steel to be well clear of the office room door, the patch of light moved out from under the cabinet, its faint fabric sound making tiny echoes in the empty room. The patch of light moved away from the coldness of the freezer. It then waited.

Chapter Thirteen

It was evening again by the time they had straightened the kitchen and the last of the books and pictures had been burned.

The house was still quiet and there were no further happenings on the second floor landing, apart from the whispered voice that chanted incessantly from behind the closed, cupboard-stair door.

'*Poor thing, Poor thing, Poor thing, Poor thing . . .*'

Lead had maintained his watch on the landing, except for one brief spell when he had been called down to the kitchen to eat his usual enormous meal and to help Steel patch up the outside door and the broken window.

It was during a part of this spell, during the two or three minutes that it took for Rob to relieve Lead on the landing, that the other two patches of light had moved out from under the cupboard-stair door. They had moved swiftly, and with a sense of purpose, down the two flights of stairs and into the hallway. Once there, they had paused for a moment, as if to listen to the voices in the kitchen. The patches of light had then glided quickly to the cellar door, slipped beneath it and moved on down the stone steps to the darkness of the winding cellar.

When Lead had returned to the upstairs landing, accompanied by Steel, Rob was left alone in the kitchen. Sapphire and Helen were making up the two temporary beds in the sitting-room, and it was left to Rob to sweep the kitchen floor now that the room had been more or less set to rights.

Rob was close to the office lobby, sweeping the last few leaves and pieces of broken china from the corners of the kitchen, when he heard the slight, sharp click of the office door catch. He set down the broom and moved into the lobby to look.

The office door was slightly ajar, by about two or three inches, as if the catch had slipped and allowed the door to open.

Rob stared at the door for a moment. He then moved towards it and listened.

There was no sound from inside the office, other than the steady hum of the freezer motor.

The cold air was escaping from the room. Rob shivered slightly as he felt it, and he reached out to close the office door. Then something, some clear-cut, sensible thought entered his head and told him that he ought not to.

Rob withdrew his hand. As he did so, a second well-defined thought appeared in his head. The thought stated that it was perfectly reasonable and natural for him to enter the office room.

Rob reached out once more, opened the door and entered the cold office.

The figure of a man was standing in the darkness at the corner of the room.

Rob turned on the light, quickly.

The man stood there, looking relaxed and almost at home in the icy, empty room. He was even smiling as he looked at Rob.

Rob stared at the figure of his father. 'Dad!' he cried out.

His father continued to smile warmly. 'Hallo, Rob,' he said.

Rob stood there in the doorway, unsure. His first reactions, on seeing his father once more, were those of shock and pleasure. Yet something was wrong. He was not sure yet, but something *had* to be wrong. Although to turn and run now, to call for help seemed, in Rob's confused state, equally wrong. In a way, it would have been an act of betrayal. Whether he was looking at an image, or even a ghost, it was still the figure of his father, whom he loved and needed, that stood there in this lonely room. And that mattered. Therefore there was time to stand there, time to look. And that also seemed natural to him. That also mattered.

'What— what are you doing in here, Dad?' he eventually managed to ask. And he was half expecting, perhaps even dreading, that this representation of his father would now vanish, would be just another cruel trick, like the voice of his mother that had called to him through the attic room.

But his father did not vanish. 'Well why shouldn't I be here?' he answered instead, with the same friendly smile.

'But you disappeared, Dad.'

'Disappeared?' His father chuckled slightly, patiently. 'What are you talking about, disappeared?'

And it made sense. The very tone of the voice made it down-to-earth common sense. Rob found himself agreeing. 'Why should his father have disappeared?'

'Come in and close the door, Rob. There's a good lad.'

'Close it?'

'Yes. Close it.'

And his father walked across the room and quickly closed the office door himself. He closed it quietly, still smiling at Rob as he did so.

Outside, in the kitchen, Rob could hear the voices of Sapphire and Helen entering.

'But why do we have to close the door, Dad?' And a faint shiver went through him as he asked the question. A shiver that was deeper and more searching than the feeling of coldness.

'Ssh!' Rob's father put his finger to his lips.

'I mean, everything's alright now, isn't it, now that you're back with us?'

But Rob's father did not answer. He was listening at the door.

'Anyway, it's cold in here Dad. It's freezing.'

'Is it?' His father seemed to think about it. 'Oh, yes. I suppose it is.'

Rob felt the inner shiver again as he said anxiously, 'I want you to open that door please, Dad.'

Rob's father stared at him for a moment, the smile leaving his face.

'Or I can open it myself. Either that or I can shout.'

'Why should you want to shout?'

Rob turned towards the door.

'Alright, Rob. I should have known, I suppose.'

There was a change in his father's voice that made Rob turn to look. His father's face had a slightly pained, resigned expression upon it. And it was an expression that Rob had known of old. His mother would always refer to it as, 'Your father's sulky look. He can't get his own way.' But Rob had often disagreed with her, privately. He had always read that look differently. His mother was a very outward person. If she was upset, she would show it, she would let the entire house know it. Not in an angry way but in a theatrical way that was almost flamboyant with gestures and protests. She could hold the floor, grab their attention and amuse them in any way she chose. And she knew it.

But, with his father it was different. Rob knew when he was hurt, when the man felt misunderstood. Rob knew the look. An undemonstrative, almost sad look. And Rob's father had that look now.

'Should have known what?' asked Rob.

'Well, that I'd be wasting my time trying to fool you.' And his father shrugged slightly and moved away to the far side of the office, as far away from the door as possible. 'Go on, then,' he said, 'Open the door.'

Rob hesitated for a moment and then reached out slowly for the door handle.

'Call out for your so-called friends,' his father went on. 'That way, you really *will* put me in danger.'

His hand still resting on the handle of the door, Rob stared at his father.

'Rob?' Sapphire's voice called faintly from out in the hallway somewhere. 'Where are you, Rob?' Then a silence, as if Sapphire had gone in search of him.

'Put you in danger?' Rob asked the lonely figure that stood in the corner of the room.

'Yes. But not only me. Your mother as well. And yourself.'

'And Helen?'

'Oh, yes. And Helen,' he said, although Rob did not notice, just a little too quickly.

The coldness of the room made Rob's face feel stiff. His hand, still resting on the door handle, felt almost frozen. But he waited, still watching his father.

'Because I— well, I didn't really disappear, Rob.'

'Didn't disappear? But you . . .'

'I've been here in the house all the time.' His father smiled again, but it was a dispirited, apologetic kind of smile. 'I've been hiding.'

'Hiding?'

'Yes.'

Rob considered it. In a way, it made a kind of sense to him. He could not understand it, but at least the explanation seemed somehow believable.

'And Mum? What about Mum?'

'She's been with me. We've both been hiding.'

'But why?'

His father looked at him steadily. 'Don't you know why?'

'Yes,' said Rob, 'Because the house is being threatened by . . .'

'By them,' his fathered interrupted quickly.

'Them?'

'As I've said, I could never fool you, Rob.' His father moved slowly back into the centre of the room and stood by the converted cabinet with its sheet of heavy iced-up glass. 'But *they've* fooled you.'

Rob thought about it for a moment and then realised what his father meant. Glancing first at the door, Rob looked back at his father.

'Sapphire and Steel?'

'Yes.' His father nodded seriously. 'They're the real danger, the real threat. Nothing else is.'

And a series of unanswered questions sped through Rob's mind, like the flicked pages of an unread book. The arrival of Steel and Sapphire, Constable Daly, the nailed-up room, the ship that had been sunk.

'Had you never once stopped to think, Rob?' His father was saying. 'Never once wondered about them?'

Very slowly, Rob removed his hand from the door.

8

'I thought he was with you.'

Sapphire was standing at the foot of the stairs with Helen close beside her.

'No.' Steel walked down the stairs, followed by Lead.

'But we left him in the kitchen,' said Sapphire, 'That was the last time we saw him.'

Steel looked along the hallway, towards the kitchen.

The second and third patches of light waited in the dark cellar. There were no pictures or books left in the house, but the patches of light had found something that was just as good, perhaps even better. And so they waited, beyond the old support beams and wooden stanchions that jutted and straddled like dead trees, at the very far end of the cellar.

'Rob!' Sapphire called as she entered the kitchen, followed by Steel, Lead and Helen.

There was no answer.

Rob and his father listened as Sapphire called out a second time.

'Rob?' A question now. A trace of urgency in her voice.

Putting his finger to his lips once more, Rob's father moved slowly towards Rob and the office door.

'Now you must trust me, Rob.'

Rob looked at his father and nodded.

'I need you to help me.' His father spoke quietly and secretively, aware of the noises and the voices outside in the kitchen.

'Of course, Dad, but . . .

'I want you to come with me.' Rob's father held out his hand.

Rob looked at the extended hand, but made no attempt to take the hand in his.

'Your mother and I, we really need your help, Rob.'

'Mother.' Rob thought of her, there in the strange, cold atmosphere of the room. He thought of the sense of fun that she provided when she was in one of her frequently good moods.

He remembered her vitality, the spontaneous games, the jokes, the fun and the laughter, all generated by her sometimes wild charm. And suddenly it seemed right that Dad would be here asking for help. Not her. It was not like her to be the one who brought the warnings, or to have to talk in such a furtive, pleading fashion. Dad, yes. But not her. And so it seemed right.

'Wouldn't you like to see her?' Rob's father's hand was still extended, still waiting. 'Wouldn't you like to see your mother?'

'Of course I would,' said Rob, eagerly.

And his father smiled again, pleased. 'Come on, then. I'll take you to her.'

'Where is she?'

'I told you. Hiding.'

'But where?'

'In the cellar,' said Rob's father, his hand still reaching out. 'She's waiting there for you.'

Rob stared at his father, and at the hand that was held out to him.

'She's waiting to see you, Rob.'

With his mind filled with the thoughts of his mother, Rob raised his hand just a fraction. As he did so, his father reached forward, the smile still there on his face, and took Rob's hand.

Looking into the reassuring eyes of his father, Rob failed to see the pale glow of light that spread across his father's hand and into his own.

Sapphire had realised that there was something wrong in the office room. Apart from outside the house, or maybe in the cellar, there was no other place where Rob was likely to have been. Then, moving into the office lobby, she had sensed it.

'In there,' she said, moving back from the door and reaching to protect Helen.

Steel and Lead moved quickly into the lobby and advanced on the office door. Like something they were well practised in, they gave, and took, no instructions from each other as Steel moved to the side of the door and Lead walked straight at it. He raised his giant hands as he walked and hit the door with the flat of them. The door was lifted and driven inwards, ripping out its hinges and catch as it crashed into the room.

Steel moved quickly, moving over the fallen door before the dust even had time to hover, let alone settle.

Apart from the freezer cabinet, the office was empty.

As Rob's father took him by the hand, Rob was half aware that the room was different, that it was somehow furnished again. He thought he could see the desk, the bookshelves, the swivel-chair. But these things were only vaguely glimpsed, like objects seen through tired eyes.

In fact, Rob felt very tired and heavy-eyed as his father opened the office door and led him through the lobby and into the kitchen.

The kitchen was deserted, and, because of his half-awake state, Rob thought he could see the room as it was before the strong wind had burst through and wrecked it. But he felt far too weary to have to try and think about it.

He tried to keep his feet steady as his father led the way across the deserted kitchen.

Steel and Lead had walked back over the broken door, then through the lobby and into the kitchen. There they stopped.

Sapphire was standing in the centre of the room. Her head turned slowly as she 'tested', with raised hand, the room's atmosphere.

'There's something in here, Steel,' she said, turning and scanning the room with her hands. 'Crossing the room. Passing through it.'

'Malevolent?' asked Steel.

'Part of it, yes.' Sapphire swivelled her hands through the air of the room. 'It's about— let me see, I'd say about three days out of time.'

'Forward or backwards?'

Sapphire's hands swung slowly to follow an imaginary path that led to the hallway door. 'In past time,' was her calculation. 'Yes, it's moving on a mirror-line.'

'How great?' asked Steel, following the movement of Sapphire's hands and measuring an imaginary beam.

'An echo-sequence, that's all,' said Sapphire, 'A visual echo.'

Steel continued to move across the room, like a man on stepping-stones. Lead walked with him, keeping close.

'And you can't cut in on it?' Lead suggested.

Sapphire shook her head. 'No. Too far back for me.' She then stopped, her hands directed at the hallway door. 'It's gone now. Yes, it's gone.'

She lowered her hands.

'Where's Rob?' asked Helen. 'Where is he?'

But no-one answered. Steel and Lead were hurrying back to the office room as Sapphire moved warily towards the hallway door.

Rob still felt in a tired, sleep-like state as his father guided him along the hallway to the cellar door.

His father opened the door and they stepped down on to the dank, stone steps of the cellar, closing the door to after them.

The steps were steep, and the cellar itself was more like a series of low passageways that twisted their way under the house.

But Rob did not feel scared any more as his father led the way through the darkness of the cellar that was lit only by the few small overhead gratings. The sleepiness was like an anaesthetic. All Rob cared about was the fact that he was with his father and soon he would see his mother.

And he was reminded of other days, other evenings. When he was younger. When he was a small boy and it was holiday time. It would be dusk, growing into evening, and his father would be walking him back to the holiday chalet. There would be lights on in windows, and it would be late, well past his time

117

for going to bed. But it was the summer, and it was a holiday, and no matter how tired he felt in the warm evening air, he would be comforted by the knowledge that his father would be taking him to some strange, but bright and cosy room where his mother would be waiting.

So this was like it, this walk through the cellar. These were the same hazy, safe feelings. Therefore there could be nothing to worry about, he told himself.

Chapter Fourteen

'Lift it!' Steel shouted the words like a command.

Lead seized the heavy sheet of glass and swung it up from the top of the cabinet. Sapphire was waiting in the hallway with Helen as Steel and Lead came out from the kitchen.

Steel's face was tense. 'It's gone,' he announced. 'The patch of light has gone.'

There was no surprise on Sapphire's face, only a look of seriousness that matched the expression of Steel's. 'And I think I know where it's gone,' she said as she turned to face the cellar door.

Moving on instinct, Lead hit the cellar door in the same way that he had gained entry to the office. The cellar door caved inwards under the impact.

Rob and his father were halfway across the cellar, moving around boxes and cases and old pieces of furniture, when one stray thought, perhaps triggered by what seemed the faraway sound of the breaking door, entered Rob's mind.

'I've been— I've been down here a lot of times since you and Mum disappeared,' he said, but his father did not answer as they threaded their way through the cellar towards the end section.

'So why haven't I seen you?'

'Seen us?' his father asked, still leading Rob by his hand.

'Yes. Why haven't I seen you? I mean, there aren't that many places to hide, down here.'

'No places, no. But there are ways.'

'Ways?' Rob asked, sleepily.

'Ways of hiding. I'll show you.'

Sapphire's voice echoed through the narrow alleyways of the cellar. 'Ro-ob!'

And then Steel's voice. 'Rob?'

Some reflex made Rob halt as the voices floated through his tired mind, like the voices of faceless people in a dream.

'Are you down there, Rob?'

His father tightened the grip on his hand. 'Don't listen to them,' he whispered. 'We'll soon be safe.'

Helen had been told to sit at the top of the cellar steps, and to stay there, while Steel, Sapphire and Lead made their way down the steps to the cellar itself. They peered through at the darkness, Sapphire glancing back to check on Helen as they looked and listened and exercised their senses.

The end section of the cellar was darker still. There were no gratings here to provide even a dim light. A cross-beam and two upright, sunken beams formed a kind of arch that led to the end section and the bare, blank wall beyond. The wall that was the very end of the house.

Rob's father led the way to the beams and then stopped.

'Where is she?' Rob peered lazily into the darkness beyond the beams. 'Where's Mum?'

Rob's father said nothing.

'I can't see her,' said Rob.

'Look.' His father pointed towards the shadowy end wall of the house. 'There she is.'

- In the corner of the end section, a dark shape seemed to detach itself from the matching darkness.

Rob stared through tired eyes. He could just about define the shape as the shadowed figure of a woman. But her head was lowered, and it was turned away from him. Her long hair hung down like dark curtains.

'Mum?' Rob said, smiling a weary but pleased smile.

'Hello, Rob,' murmured the dark shape, its head still lowered, still turned away.

'There you are,' Rob's father said, moving towards the beams, towards the dark shape, taking Rob with him.

Again, some hidden reflex, the same tiny scrap of spirit that had made Rob question his mother's voice at the attic room door, nagged away inside him. And so he held back from the beams that seemed to lead nowhere.

The grip was tightened on Rob's hand as his father asked, 'Come on, you wanted to see her, didn't you?'

'Yes, but . . .'

'But what?'

Rob tried to focus his eyes on the dark shape that resembled his mother, and yet chose to look away.

'Well, why— why doesn't she look at us?'

Rob's father stood there for a moment, as if to consider the question. He then spoke to the figure. 'Yes, dear. Why won't you look at us?'

The figure raised its head very slowly and then turned its body, equally slowly, to face Rob.

The figure had no face. No features. There was only a darkness under the strands of hair, where a face should have been. Just a blackness. A nothingness.

Rob screamed loudly, and the tiredness suddenly left him. But it was far too late. Whatever this thing was, that pretended to be his father, it was dragging him past the beams and into the end section of the cellar.

At the sound of the scream, Steel, Sapphire and Lead ran quickly through the cluttered passageways of the cellar.

When they eventually reached the arched support beams, and were ready to move on past them, Sapphire stopped suddenly, her arms extended like a barrier.

'Wait.'

Steel and Lead waited.

'Just— just there.' Sapphire's hands moved, testing the area around the beams. 'Beyond those wooden beams.'

Steel nodded and took a half pace forward. 'We're alright as far as the beams?' he asked.

'Yes.'

'What about the beams themselves?' said Steel, taking another half pace forward.

'No!'

Steel checked himself in mid-action and moved back one pace, watching Sapphire as he did so.

'It's where it starts,' said Sapphire, 'Somewhere.'

'In the beams?'

'Somewhere.' Sapphire was still testing. 'Here somewhere. These beams are a part of it.'

Steel nodded, and Sapphire relaxed and moved back slightly from the archway of beams.

Moving from one side of the cellar wall to the other, Steel studied the space between the beams as if he were looking closely at some invisible texture. He then looked beyond the wooden supports and into the end section.

Rob was not there. Neither was his father, nor the shadowed figure.

Steel waited for a moment and then called, 'Rob?'

'Yes— yes, Steel?' Rob's voice answered back from the empty section of the cellar.

The moment that Rob had been pulled past the beams, things had changed abruptly. He had found himself alone and in full command of his senses. He also felt very lost and frightened.

He had immediately realised that he was no longer in the house. He was outside somewhere. But where? It was still night and he had looked around him, as far as he could see, on a night that was quite cloudy with very little moonlight.

The wind blew in, unbroken, across what seemed to be open land. And Rob had recognised it as the very same wind, coming in from the bay, that blew ceaselessly past the house.

But the house was not there anymore.

Then, adjusting to the darkness, he had looked at the ground

122

around his feet. He had then found that he was standing on a flagstone floor that was surrounded by a comparatively shallow, rectangular trench. There were a few rough building stones set into the trench and, here and there, some pegs and posts set out like markers. Then, he had looked up and seen the two upright beams, freshly hewn and fixed temporarily into place.

And the night air was different. It smelled and tasted somehow clearer.

He had kept his position, the same position that he had been in when the image of his father and the shadowed figure had vanished, leaving him there alone, because he knew that to stay exactly as he was standing was important.

But he had moved his head. He had wanted to try to look out towards Scars Edge. The lights of the village could always be seen reflected against the night sky, especially when there was low cloud.

So he had moved his head carefully. He then saw, close at hand, some old, heavy-looking building tools and a wheelbarrow that resembled a wooden tub. He had then looked out in the direction of Scars Edge.

The wind was the same, and so was the faint sound of the sea. But there were no comforting lights at a distance. Scars Edge was not there.

And then he had realised why he was outside in the night air. The village of Scars Edge had probably not been thought of— yet. And his house, the old house that he lived in, was only just about to be built.

He had then moved his head back quickly and maintained his original position. He was very frightened, and had been relieved to hear Steel's voice so close at hand.

'I— I know what to do, Steel,' he called out to the night air.

Steel's voice answered, still close by. 'Tell me, Rob.'

'Well, this is— this is what happened to Sapphire, isn't it? Like on the landing?'

'Yes.'

123

'So I— so I know what to do, Steel. I just stand very still, don't I?'

There was no answer and Rob felt a sudden surge of panic. 'Don't I?' he called out again, louder this time.

Steel's voice answered quickly. 'Yes, Rob, you do. And that's good. That's very good, Rob. You're doing the right thing.'

And Rob smiled a little, nervously. Just a pleased smile to himself. Being praised by Steel, that was something. Then, calling out again, he said, 'I'm sorry, Steel, but it was my father.'

'Your father?' Steel's voice came back to him through the fresh, clear air.

'Yes. He brought me down here, down into the cellar—well, not really him.'

A moment passed, as if Steel was busy thinking things out, back there in the proper time. And Rob wanted to be there. He was sorry that he had mistrusted them. He was sorry for so many things. And yet he felt that he had tried. Had tried his best, in his own way.

'Whatever it was that was pretending to be your father,' said Steel's voice, 'Is it with you now?'

Rob sensed some anxiety in the voice. 'No,' he called back, 'I'm alone here.'

Once again, Steel answered quickly. 'You're not alone, Rob.'

'No.' Rob whispered.

'Did you hear that?'

'Yes.'

'You're quite close to us, Rob.' It was Sapphire's voice this time.

'Yes, Sapphire.'

Sapphire spoke again. 'We're all here in the cellar and you're one of us.'

Then Lead spoke, the deep voice booming its reassurance. 'Yes, you're with us, boy. You're right here with us.'

And Rob felt the cool wind blowing in across this open, alien landscape. Two hundred years back in time, and he was there like something that did not belong, something that was not protected, like a caged bird let loose into a vast open territory that it did not know and was not equipped for.

And everything, the fear, the hurt, the anxiety for his parents, plus the confusion and the false, fake hopes, all seemed to shift uncontrollably inside him.

Rob began to cry.

Steel and Sapphire, watched by Lead, stood in the dark cellar and listened to the sound of Rob crying.

Beckoning to Sapphire, Steel turned away, so that he could not be heard by the unseen Rob.

'Is he in danger?' Steel asked, quietly.

'Yes.' Sapphire nodded, keeping her voice low. 'He's in great danger.'

Steel looked at her, then glanced back at the wooden beams and the empty, shadowy section of the cellar.

Lead had heard. He watched them, a set look on his face.

'You see, he's not really alone in there.' Sapphire whispered, 'Something's in there with him.'

It was a moment or two before Steel moved back to face the wall again. 'Rob?' he called.

'Yes?' Rob spoke, swallowing hard, trying to hide his tears.

'Can you describe where you are to me? Without moving from your position, can you do that?'

'Yes,' said Rob's voice, 'I've already looked.'

'And?'

'And I'm in the cellar. The end of the cellar. Well— part of it, I suppose.'

'Part of it?'

'Yes. It's the cellar, but it isn't finished.'

Steel looked at Sapphire, then at Lead, then back to the arched beams.

'It's being built.' Rob's voice spoke out from the emptiness once more. 'It's the house, but it's— it isn't here yet. It's being built. Only just being built. I can see the foundations. There's— there's no-one here. It's night time, you see. They must have all gone home.'

'Alright, Rob,' said Steel, 'Now just be patient, will you?'

'Yes,' was the choked reply.

'There's no need to cry and there's no need to worry.'

'I'm not crying,' Rob's voice said quickly.

'Good. Now just be patient and leave it to us.' Steel then turned to Lead. 'The other child,' he said, 'She's still on her own.'

Lead nodded and ambled back down the cellar passageways towards the stairs, ducking his head under the low sections of ceiling as he went.

Steel had turned to Sapphire once more. 'The house being built?' he asked quietly, 'Why should it take him back there?'

'Because whatever's in there has chosen it.'

'The patches of light?'

Sapphire nodded. 'Most probably, yes.'

'How many of them?'

'I don't know.'

Steel glanced towards the end section of the cellar once more, then back. 'But they need something to lock on to, don't they?' he said. 'I mean, I can't imagine pictures being hung, or rhymes being said, in a house that isn't even built.'

'All the same, they must be in there.'

Steel looked steadily at Sapphire for a moment. 'Right,' he said, turning back to face the end section, 'Let's locate them.'

'Rob?'

Sapphire's voice spoke from out of the night, from the cellar, from the house that he was no longer in, no longer a part of.

'Yes?' Rob answered, glad of the sound of the voice in this lonely place.

'Those patches of light, Rob.' Sapphire tried to make it sound as casual as possible under the circumstances. 'Remember them?'

'Yes.'

Then there was a pause, and Rob waited anxiously to hear the voice again.

'Well they're— they're probably in there with you, Rob.'

126

Rob swallowed hard.

'Rob?' Sapphire's voice called quickly, urgently.

'Yes— yes, I heard,' said Rob. He moved his head to look around him at the darkness.

'So therefore we must find them, Rob. We must find those patches of light.'

'Find them?' For a moment, Rob thought that he would be asked to search for the patches of light. He experienced a cold feeling of fear.

Sapphire's voice rang out again. 'So I'm going to make them appear, Rob.'

'Oh,' replied Rob, swallowing hard once more, but feeling slightly relieved.

'Now when you see them,' Sapphire's voice continued with its instructions, 'Just tell us. Call out quickly and give us their locations from where you are. Understand?'

'Yes,' said Rob, weakly.

The cool sound of Steel's voice penetrated the thin, high sound of the wind. 'Any moment now, Rob.'

Rob waited, feeling like someone who was fixed to a spot. Fixed there forever. His mind was filled with a jumble of thoughts. Perhaps this was the time-corridor thing. This place. A nowhere place. Perhaps he was to be left here now. Perhaps it would never be morning, and never be night again. Perhaps it would always stay like this, the very same time. So therefore he would never feel hungry, never feel tired, never feel anything but this strange sense of isolation, of not belonging. Perhaps it would be like that for him forever.

Then Sapphire's clear eyes, like a bright, but cool, summer sky, seemed to appear before him, as if the look from those eyes was capable of spanning time and distance.

And he felt suddenly better, those eyes were relaying a kind of message, like a signal, like a flag of recognition.

Then he saw the first patch of light appear.

Rob turned his head quickly. The patch of light was glowing faintly, as if trying not to be seen. It was situated in the spot where he had last seen the false image of his father.

'It's here,' shouted Rob.

Steel saw the patch of light glowing in the darkness at the end of the cellar.

With eyes opened, Sapphire stood, trance-like, facing the end section.

'Yes, I see it,' called Steel, 'Stay still.'

As he spoke, another patch of light flickered and glowed in the far corner where the dark figure had once stood.

'And another one,' Rob's voice cried out, 'Just behind me. Can you see it?'

'Yes. I can see it. Now do you remember the patch of light that trapped Sapphire?'

'Of course I do.' Rob's voice replied.

'Fine.' Steel's face was tense. 'Now that patch of light got into a picture.' Then before Rob could answer, 'Now look quickly, Rob. Tell me what those two patches of light have chosen. Tell me now!'

Steel waited.

'Nothing, Steel,' was Rob's eventual reply.

'Nothing?'

'No. Well, nothing that means much.'

'Tell me!' Steel almost shouted the words.

Hounded by Steel's questions, Rob seemed to have forgotten most of his fear. 'Well one's— one's on some earth. And the other one—well, that's on a piece of stone, an ordinary piece of stone.'

There was an angry, disappointed look on Steel's face. He relaxed slightly and was about to turn to Sapphire.

'Wait!' Sapphire's eyes were still open wide, still concentrating.

Steel looked at her and waited.

'There's another one,' said Sapphire, 'A third one.'

Steel turned to look.

The third patch of light glowed and pulsated as it struggled in its effort not to be seen. It was at the bottom corner of the cellar's end wall, flush with the floor, the flickering light shifting under the old, decayed plaster of the wall.

Out in the open air, in the small piece of time that Rob was trapped in, the third patch of light glowed in the corner of the foundations. It shone inside one of the few stones that had been laid. It was the very end stone. The corner stone. He called out, to tell Steel, then he stared at the pale luminosity of the stone. Figures and letters had been etched into its rough surface.

Leaning forward, with his feet still fixed firmly in place, Rob tried to read what had been carved into the stone.

'No, Rob.' Sapphire's voice spoke to him. 'Leave it to me.'

Steel waited as Sapphire closed her eyes and concentrated on the stone.

'It's a— it's a name,' she said as Steel watched her. 'Someone's name. Jed— Jed Mace. Second— the second of Feb— February. Seventeen—seventeen hundred and thirty-six.'

'Jed Mace?' Steel stared towards the third patch of light.

'The man who built the house.' Sapphire said, her eyes still closed. 'The stone was the first one to be laid. The writing on it, it's a kind of grace-note.'

Steel watched the three patches of light that trembled and glowed in the dark section of the cellar. Like small animals that had been cornered, they seemed to be nervously waiting, but gave the impression of being much more dangerous because of that.

'How much time?' asked Steel.

'Time?'

'Where Rob is now. How much time was used up until that stone was laid?'

Eyes still closed, Sapphire centred her mind on the stone.

'Half— half a day,' she murmured, as if echoing the voice of someone from long ago. 'Hard work— we worked hard, all of us. But half a day. Yes, a good half a day.'

Then Sapphire opened her eyes and the patches of light faded.

'It's made two mistakes,' said Steel, quietly.

'What are they?'

'No-one builds houses backwards.' Steel looked around him, and at the ceiling above him. 'And it came in at the top, didn't it? The gable?'

'Yes.' Sapphire nodded. 'The last piece of the house to be built.'

'And its second mistake was in letting its offspring hide in there. In that stone.'

Sapphire looked towards the dilapidated plaster of the end wall. 'The first piece of the house to be built.'

'Yes.' Steel studied the cellar wall for a moment or two more, then turned to walk back along the passageway. 'Think you can take it back half a day?' he asked, without turning.

Glancing first towards the end section, Sapphire moved quickly after Steel.

'Of course I can take it back half a day.'

'Good,' said Steel as he walked, 'Because we're going to bring it down.'

Sapphire stared at him.

'Bring it down into the time it's chosen.'

'So how do we get it down here?' Sapphire asked.

Steel halted in the cellar passageway. Turning to look at Sapphire, he said, 'We'll give it the next nursery-rhyme, shall we?' Then, before Sapphire could reply, he added, 'All we need is someone to act as bait.'

Sapphire stared at him yet again. But Steel was walking again, making his way towards the cellar steps. 'I'll leave you to choose an appropriate rhyme for her,' he called back.

Helen stood on the second landing like somebody who was being rehearsed. She faced the stairs, her back to the cupboard-stair door. Then, as if on cue, Helen began to recite.

'*This is the house that Jack built,*' she said, in a child's steady monotone, as she walked towards the head of the opposite stairs.

'*This is the malt that lay in the house that Jack built.*'

Helen began to descend the stairs. '*This is the rat that ate the malt, that lay in the house that Jack built,*'

The cupboard-stair door flickered into life as the small figure of Helen disappeared below the ridge of the stair.

'*This is the cat that killed the rat, that ate the malt that lay in the house that Jack built,*'

Like a flutter and a rustle, like blankets shaken busily from a window, the fabric sound began to grow in volume as the cupboard-stair door began to glow.

Helen's frail voice drifted back from the stairs. '*This is the dog, that worried the cat, that killed the rat, that ate the malt, that lay in the house that Jack built,*'

The jumbled sounds and the shapes began to jostle and spill through the very structure of the cupboard-stair door.

As Helen stepped slowly down the flight of stairs, the reflected light poured on to the walls of the landing above her.

'*This is the cow with the crumpled horn, that tossed the dog, that— that . . .*'

Helen forgot the words. She stopped on the middle step of the stairs and tried to remember them. It was difficult, and so she sat down on the step, to make remembering easier.

Steel waited at a halfway point in the cellar. His face was ashen once more, and his eyes seemed fixed as he stared ahead and waited.

Peering closely at Steel's pale face, Lead seemed satisfied. The freezing air that surrounded Steel did not seem to trouble the big man as he took his place beside Steel and waited.

Helen remembered the words. 'Oh, yes,' she said to herself, but remained sitting on the step so that she could get the words in the right order inside her mind.

The light had filled the landing above. It now began to trickle and spread down the stairs above and behind Helen.

'Helen!' It was a whispered shout from Sapphire on the landing below. 'Come on, Helen!'

Smiling, as if it was a kind of party game, Helen stood up. '*That tossed the dog, that worried the cat,*' she said, as she began to descend the stairs once more.

'That's it. That's fine,' said Sapphire, encouragingly.

And Helen smiled yet again as the light spread itself out upon the staircase wall and the shapes and figures loomed up and then down on to the steps of the stairs.

'That killed the rat, that ate the malt that lay in the house that Jack built,'

Pleased with her effort, Helen reached the landing and began to move across it as Sapphire eased herself back towards the next flight of stairs, waving Helen on as she did so.

'This is the man all tattered and torn, that kissed the maiden all forlorn . . .'

'Helen!'

Sapphire looked up. There was a dark figure on the stairs above. A shape that stood with its head lowered and its face turned away, long hair hanging down.

'Come back up the stairs, Helen . . .'

'Don't listen!' urged Sapphire.

'Time for bed.'

But Helen stopped reciting the rhyme. She halted on the landing and looked directly at Sapphire.

'Do you hear me, Helen?' the voice insisted, 'You won't have a kiss goodnight.'

Sapphire looked up at the dark figure. 'Don't look back, Helen,' she whispered, urgently. 'Please don't look back.'

'Hel-en!'

But Helen was still looking at Sapphire. 'It's not Mama, is it?' she asked.

'No,' said Sapphire with relief.

'This is the priest all shaven and shorn,' Helen seemed to have forgotten the incident already. *'That married the man all tattered and torn,'* she chanted happily as she began to descend the last flight of stairs.

'It's coming, Steel. It's coming down.' Sapphire's words entered silently into Steel's mind. He moved his head stiffly and looked along the cellar towards the distant steps.

Lead also turned to look.

They heard the footsteps of both Helen and Sapphire descending the stone steps.

'*This is the cock that crowed in the morn,*' Helen's voice echoed thinly through the cellar. '*That waked the priest all shaven and shorn,*'

Lead watched as Sapphire appeared at the entrance end of the cellar. Beyond her, the tiny figure of Helen struggled on with the rhyme and the sudden darkness of the cellar.

Then that darkness seemed to be eased slightly as the glow spilled in from the hallway and down the cellar steps.

The fabric sound, too, increased in volume now, so that Helen's voice could no longer be heard. Lead watched her as she approached, behind Sapphire, her child's mouth still uttering the words of the rhyme that no-one could hear any more.

'We're giving it the whole house?' shouted Lead over the sound.

Sapphire hurried towards him, holding on to Helen's hand now. The bright glow made silhouettes of their shapes.

'Yes, the whole house.' Sapphire shouted back.

Steel turned to face the beams and the dark end section of the cellar.

'Well, there's no way out from this cellar.' Lead complained.

'Not for us—no,' said Steel as he walked towards the beams.

Rob would never be quite sure of exactly what did happen. But he heard, as he waited in the darkness, the fabric sound. And had thought, for one frightening moment, that the thing from the attic room was travelling across the surrounding fields towards him.

Then there was a blast of icy cold air and Steel appeared beside him on the foundations of the house. Steel was followed, in turn, by Lead, then Sapphire who was holding Helen by the hand.

'It's alright, Rob.' Sapphire had smiled warmly as she reached out for Rob and pulled him to her. And Rob felt himself holding on to her with the passion and the need of a small child.

'It's alright,' she said again, 'It'll be gone.'

'Gone?' Rob exclaimed, still holding her tightly, his head pressed hard against her.

'Yes. Through that stone,' he heard her say, 'Before this house was ever built.'

Then Rob heard the sound as it rumbled and shrieked towards them, but it did not seem to matter any more. Even when the sound roared and tore at his mind and his nerves, and the light poured out on to the foundation slabs and seemed to engulf them in a kind of glowing sea, it still did not seem to matter. Not now.

And he peered through narrowed eyes as he heard Sapphire say, and he could swear to this day that it was inside his head, 'Because there will be no stone.'

Then he heard the shrill shriek as Steel drove the other patches of light into the stone. And then there was a high, fierce roar, like the mother-cry of an animal. And he saw Steel touch the stone with both hands, and, as the stone frosted and turned to ice, the shrill cries rose in pitch.

Then the whole mass of light spun and twisted into the stone. As it did so, Rob saw Lead reach down and tear the large stone from its base.

Lead squeezed the stone as if it were a block of salt. And the last thing that Rob heard, as Lead crushed the stone to fine powder, was the high, terrifying screams of the mother light and its offspring. And the light also faded as the beams and walls of the cellar seemed to spin and twist into view.

Rob ran to the top of the cupboard-stair door and on to the landing. Moving quickly, he pushed open the attic bedroom door.

The rocking-chair was rocking, but there was no-one sitting in it. There was only Helen in the room, and she was sitting on the bed, an expression of shock on her young face.

'No!' said Rob to himself. 'Please, no!'

He walked quickly back to the door and looked out.

Steel and Sapphire were standing on the landing. Lead sat on the stairs behind them.

Rob stared, open-mouthed.

Steel was holding the teddy-bear. With no expression on his face whatsoever, Steel handed the teddy-bear to Sapphire, who smiled and held it out to Rob.

'Sorry,' she said, 'We forgot something.'

Still staring, Rob took the teddy-bear from her. He looked at them, unsure, then walked back into the bedroom.

Rob handed the doll to Helen, who reached out and took it. As she did so, the doll changed position in her hands, as if her very movement itself had slipped, like a gear.

And then there were sounds in the room. Helen was laughing. Rob's mother was sitting in the rocking-chair, his father was sat in his usual place.

Rob stared at them. So penetrating was the look that the laughter and the story-telling stopped for a moment.

'What's wrong, Rob?' asked his mother.

'Nothing,' said Rob. But his mind was full of the thoughts of a blueness and of a smile that was like a cool summer sky.

The thought was like a kind of pain, he realised as he walked back to the door and looked out on to the landing.

Helen and her father were laughing again, as Rob's mother read the next rhyme, making it a kind of joke.

There was no-one on the landing.

Rob stood there, looking out. He felt the strange pain again. And he wondered what it was, and whether or not it would be with him for always.

THE END

GENERAL FICTION

		Cyril Abraham	
Δ	042607114X	THE ONEDIN LINE: THE SHIPMASTER	80p
Δ	0426132661	THE ONEDIN LINE: THE IRON SHIPS	80p
Δ	042616184X	THE ONEDIN LINE: THE HIGH SEAS	80p
Δ	0426172671	THE ONEDIN LINE: THE TRADE WINDS	80p
Δ	0352304006	THE ONEDIN LINE: THE WHITE SHIPS	90p
		Spiro T. Agnew	
	0352302550	THE CANFIELD DECISION	£1.25*
		Lynne Reid Banks	
	0352302690	MY DARLING VILLAIN	85p
		Michael J. Bird	
Δ	0352301481	WHO PAYS THE FERRYMAN?	85p
Δ	0352302747	THE APHRODITE INHERITANCE	85p
		Judy Blume	
	0352302712	FOREVER	75p*
		Barbara Brett	
	0352303441	BETWEEN TWO ETERNITIES	75p*
		Jeffrey Caine	
	0352302003	HEATHCLIFF	75p
		Ramsey Campbell	
	0352304987	THE DOLL WHO ATE HIS MOTHER	75p*
		R. Chetwynd-Hayes	
Δ	0426187539	DOMINIQUE	75p
		Jackie Collins	
Δ	0352395621	THE STUD	75p
	0352300701	LOVEHEAD	75p
	0352398663	THE WORLD IS FULL OF DIVORCED WOMEN	75p
Δ	0352398752	THE WORLD IS FULL OF MARRIED MEN	75p
		Catherine Cookson	
	0426163796	THE GARMENT	70p
	0426163524	HANNAH MASSEY	70p
	0426163605	SLINKY JANE	70p
		Tony Curtis	
	0352302194	KID ANDREW CODY AND JULIE SPARROW	95p*
		Robertson Davies	
	0352396113	FIFTH BUSINESS	95p*
	0352395281	THE MANTICORE	£1.25*
		Alexander Edwards	
Δ	0352396881	A STAR IS BORN	60p*

†For sale in Britain and Ireland only.
*Not for sale in Canada.
♦ Film & T.V. tie-ins.

GENERAL FICTION

Δ	0352303603	Henry Edwards **SGT. PEPPER'S LONELY HEARTS CLUB BAND**	75p*
	0426188330	Joy Fielding **THE TRANSFORMATION**	95p*
	0352396857	Terry Fisher **IF YOU'VE GOT THE MONEY**	70p
	0352395273	Ken Grimwood **BREAKTHROUGH**	75p*
Δ	0352304979	Robert Grossbach **CALIFORNIA SUITE**	75p*
	0352301880	D. G. Finlay **ONCE AROUND THE SUN**	95p*
Δ	0352305142	Peter J. Hammond **SAPPHIRE AND STEEL**	75p
	0426165209	Brian Hayles **SPRING AT BROOKFIELD**	70p
Δ	0352304030	William Johnston **KING**	£1.25*
		HAPPY DAYS:	
Δ	0426183746	**No. 1 THE FONZ AND LAZONGA**	70p*
Δ	0426183827	**No. 2 THE BIKE TYCOON**	70p*
Δ	0426184386	**No. 3 DEAR FONZIE . . .**	70p*
Δ	0426186222	**No. 4 FONZIE GOES TO COLLEGE**	70p*
Δ	0426187296	**No. 5 READY TO GO STEADY**	70p*
Δ	042618825X	**No. 6 FONZIE DROPS IN**	70p*
Δ	0426188764	**No. 7 THE INVADERS**	70p*
Δ	042619019X	**No. 8 FONZIE, FONZIE SUPERSTAR**	70p*
	0352303956	Heinz Konsalik **THE WAR BRIDE**	85p
	0427003210	**THE DAMNED OF THE TAIGA**	75p
Δ	0352398981	Jeffrey Konvitz **THE SENTINEL**	70p*
	0352301643	Dean R. Koontz **NIGHT CHILLS**	75p*
	0352303328	Pat McGrath **DAYBREAK**	95p

†For sale in Britain and Ireland only.
*Not for sale in Canada.
♦ Film & T.V. tie-ins.

GENERAL FICTION

Δ	0352396903	Lee Mackenzie EMMERDALE FARM (No. 1) THE LEGACY	70p
Δ	0352396296	EMMERDALE FARM (No. 2) PRODIGAL'S PROGRESS	70p
Δ	0352395974	EMMERDALE FARM (No. 3) ALL THAT A MAN HAS ...	70p
Δ	0352301414	EMMERDALE FARM (No. 4) LOVERS' MEETING	70p
Δ	0352301422	EMMERDALE FARM (No. 5) A SAD AND HAPPY SUMMER	70p
Δ	0352302437	EMMERDALE FARM (No. 6) A SENSE OF RESPONSIBILITY	70p
Δ	0352303034	EMMERDALE FARM (No. 7) NOTHING STAYS THE SAME	70p
Δ	0352303344	EMMERDALE FARM (No. 8) THE COUPLE AT DEMDYKE ROW	70p
Δ	0352302569	ANNIE SUGDEN'S COUNTRY DIARY (illus)	£1.25
Δ	0352396164	Graham Masterton THE MANITOU	70p*
	0352395265	THE DJINN	75p*
	0352302178	THE SPHINX	75p*
	0352395982	PLAGUE	75p*
	0352396911	A MILE BEFORE MORNING	75p*
	0352301562	N. Richard Nash EAST WIND, RAIN	95p*
	0352395060	CRY MACHO	95p*
	0352303778	THE LAST MAGIC (Export only) Excluding Aust., N.Z., S.A.	£1.50*
	0352302720	Anaïs Nin DELTA OF VENUS	95p*
	0352303271	Alan Parker PUDDLES IN THE LANE	70p
	0352300809	Molly Parkin LOVE ALL	70p
	0352397179	UP TIGHT	70p
	0352302151	GOOD GOLLY MS MOLLY (illus) NF	£1.25
	0352302631	SWITCHBACK	75p
Δ	0426190866	Larry Pryce THIRD TIME UNLUCKY	75p
Δ	0426189647	FINGERS	60p

†For sale in Britain and Ireland only.
*Not for sale in Canada.
♦ Film & T.V. tie-ins.

GENERAL FICTION

	0352303913	Maria Isabel Rodriguez **THE OLIVE GROVES OF ALHORA**	95p
	0352396946	Judith Rossner **TO THE PRECIPICE**	85p*
	0352302089	**NINE MONTHS IN THE LIFE OF AN OLD MAID**	75p*
	0352301465	**ANY MINUTE I CAN SPLIT**	95p*
	0352302135	Lawrence Sanders **THE PLEASURES OF HELEN**	95p*
Δ	0352302593	Pierre Sichel **THE JERSEY LILY**	95p*
	0352398892	Alan Sillitoe **THE GENERAL**	70p
	0352300965	**THE LONELINESS OF THE LONG-DISTANCE RUNNER**	85p
	0352300949	**MEN, WOMEN AND CHILDREN**	50p
	0352300981	**SATURDAY NIGHT AND SUNDAY MORNING**	70p
	0352395141	**THE WIDOWER'S SON**	85p
	0352397144	**THE FLAME OF LIFE**	85p
	0352398809	**THE RAGMAN'S DAUGHTER**	50p
	035230202X	**A START IN LIFE**	95p
	0352301821	**RAW MATERIAL**	95p
	0352302518	**KEY TO THE DOOR**	£1.50
	0352303263	**THE DEATH OF WILLIAM POSTERS**	95p
	0352303379	**A TREE ON FIRE**	£1.35
Δ	0352302402	Sylvester Stallone **PARADISE ALLEY**	75p*
Δ	0352397403	Robert Stone **DOG SOLDIERS**	95p*
Δ	0352302968	Kathleen Tynan **AGATHA**	75p*
	035230183X	Dorothy Uhnak **POLICEWOMAN**	75p*
	0352395427	Peter Upton **GREEN HILL FAR AWAY**	95p
	0352301570	Margaret Walker **JUBILEE**	95p*

† For sale in Britain and Ireland only.
* Not for sale in Canada.
♦ Film & T.V. tie-ins.

GENERAL NON-FICTION

	Lynn Barber	
0426086511	**HOW TO IMPROVE YOUR MAN IN BED**	60p
	Linda Blandford	
0352301392	**OIL SHEIKHS**	95p
	Anthony Cave Brown	
0352396121	**BODYGUARD OF LIES (Large Format)**	£1.95*
	Rodney Dale and Joan Gray	
035230345X	**EDWARDIAN INVENTIONS (large format illus)**	£1.95
	John Dean	
0352301368	**BLIND AMBITION**	£1.00*
	Dr Fitzhugh Dodson	
0352300124	**HOW TO PARENT**	75p*
	Trevor Donald	
0426190009	**CONFESSIONS OF IDI AMIN**	95p†
	Mary Dunkin	
0352304731	**ONE HUNDRED AND FORTY FOUR PICTURE POSTCARDS OF HER MAJESTY QUEEN ELIZABETH II AND HER FAMILY**	£1.95
0352301457	**THE FAMILY DICTIONARY OF SYMPTOMS**	95p*
	H. R. Haldeman	
0352303247	**THE ENDS OF POWER**	95p*
	Paul Hammond and Patrick Hughes	
0352302674	**UPON THE PUN (illus)**	£1.25
	Clive Harold	
0352303506	**THE UNINVITED**	95p
	Xaviera Hollander	
0426168623	**THE HAPPY HOOKER**	80p*
0426163443	**LETTERS TO THE HAPPY HOOKER**	80p*
0426168038	**XAVIERA GOES WILD**	80p*
0426166787	**XAVIERA ON THE BEST PART OF A MAN**	80p*
0426134265	**XAVIERA!**	80p*
	Xaviera Hollander & Marilyn Chambers	
042617996X	**XAVIERA MEETS MARILYN CHAMBERS**	80p*
	Anne Fletcher	
0352303891	**THE HAPPY HOOKER GOES TO WASHINGTON (F)**	90p*
	Georg von Konrat	
0352396032	**PASSPORT TO TRUTH**	75p
	Sharon Lawrence	
0352301627	**SO YOU WANT TO BE A ROCK & ROLL STAR**	95p*
	David Lewis	
0426087232	**SEXPIONAGE**	70p
0426087151	**THE SECRET LIFE OF ADOLF HITLER**	75p

† For sale in Britain and Ireland only
*Not for sale in Canada.
♦ Film & T.V tie-ins

GENERAL NON-FICTION

	0426086864	Linda Lovelace **INSIDE LINDA LOVELACE**	60p
	0426086945	**THE INTIMATE DIARY OF LINDA LOVELACE**	60p
	0352302704	Peter Mayle **WILL I LIKE IT?** (large format illus)	£1.95*
	0352304790	Judith Midgley-Carver and Amanda Duckett **CAREER CHOICES**	70p
	035239692X	Henry Miller **THE WORLD OF SEX**	60p
	0352302151	Molly Parkin **GOOD GOLLY MS MOLLY** (see also under General Fiction)	£1.25
Δ	0352304529	David Petrou **THE MAKING OF SUPERMAN**	75p*
	0352301449	J. B. Priestley **MAN AND TIME**	£1.50*
	0352395311	Neville Randall & Gary Keane **FOCUS ON FACT:** **THE WORLD OF INVENTION** (illus)	75p
	035239532X	**THE STORY OF SPORT** (illus)	75p
	035239529X	**THE PSYCHIC WORLD** (illus)	75p
	0352395303	**THE STORY OF CHRISTMAS** (illus)	75p
	0352395338	**UNSOLVED MYSTERIES** (illus)	75p
	0352395346	**THE STORY OF FLIGHT** (illus)	75p
	0426181638	Suze Randall **SUZE**	75p*
Δ	0352302410	Esther Ranen **THAT'S LIFE** (Large Format)	£1.95
	0352303387	Dr Benjamin Spock **BABY AND CHILD CARE**	£1.50†
	0352303670	John Walsh **THE SHROUD**	75p*
	0352303786	Dr Burton L. White **THE FIRST THREE YEARS OF LIFE**	£1.25*
	0426141970	Erna Wright **THE NEW CHILDBIRTH**	75p
	0426067282	**THE NEW CHILDHOOD**	75p
	0426054938	**PERIODS WITHOUT PAIN**	60p

†For sale in Britain and Ireland only
*Not for sale in Canada.
♦ Film & T.V. tie-ins

THRILLERS

Δ	0352303077	**DICK BARTON SPECIAL AGENT** Mike Dorrell **No. 1: THE GREAT TOBACCO CONSPIRACY**	60p
Δ	0352303085	**No. 2: THE MYSTERY OF THE MISSING FORMULA**	60p
Δ	352303093	Alan Radnor **No. 3: THE CASE OF THE VANISHING HOUSE**	60p
Δ	0352303107	Larry Pryce **No. 4: THE GOLD BULLION SWINDLE**	60p
	0352396474	Paul Bonnecarrère **ULTIMATUM**	95p
	0352302607	**THE GOLDEN TRIANGLE**	95p
	0352396059	Richard Butler **WHERE ALL THE GIRLS ARE SWEETER**	60p
	0352395354	**ITALIAN ASSETS**	75p
	0352396067	Henry Denker **THE PHYSICIANS**	95p*
	0352300523	**A PLACE FOR THE MIGHTY**	75p*
	0352303522	**THE EXPERIMENT**	95p*
	0352302127	Robert Early **A TIME OF MADNESS**	75p
	0426184548	John Gardner **THE LIQUIDATOR**	60p
	0352398582	Burt Hirschfeld **'FATHER PIG'**	60p*
	0352395176	**SECRETS**	95p*
	0427004306	William Hughes **SPLIT ON RED**	95p
	0352396253	Tony Kenrick **THE SEVEN DAY SOLDIERS**	75p*
	0352301643	Dean R. Koontz **NIGHT CHILLS**	75p*
	0426186141	Malachy McCoy **KODIAK!**	60p
	0352300078	Lawrence Sanders **THE FIRST DEADLY SIN**	95p*
	0352395435	Robert Vacha **THE OPEC PROJECT**	75p
	035230247X	**REQUIEM FOR A CROWN**	75p
	0352302585	**MOSCOW 1980**	95p
	0352303530	**THE BLACK ORCHESTRA**	95p

†For sale in Britain and Ireland only.
*Not for sale in Canada.
♦ Film & T.V. tie-ins.

NICK CARTER

0426190785	THE ARAB PLAGUE	70p*
0426168976	AZTEC AVENGER	60p*
0352304685	A BULLET FOR FIDEL	70p*
0426173635	BERLIN	60p*
0352304669	CAMBODIA	70p*
0426173554	THE COBRA KILL	60p*
0426143302	THE CODE	60p*
0352304804	CODE NAME WEREWOLF	70p*
0426185935	COUNTERFEIT AGENT	60p*
0426189485	DEATH MESSAGE: OIL 74-2	60p*
0352304812	THE DEATH STRAIN	70p*
0352304820	THE DEATH'S HEAD CONSPIRACY	70p*
0352304839	THE DEFECTOR	70p*
0352304847	THE EXECUTIONERS	70p*
0426189213	THE FANATICS OF AL ASAD	70p*
0426186818	THE GREEN WOLF CONNECTION	60p*
0352304693	THE HOUR OF THE WOLF	70p*
0352304855	THE HUMAN TIME BOMB	70p*
042607341X	ICE BOMB ZERO	70p
042618470X	THE JERUSALEM FILE	60p*
0426176545	THE KATMANDU CONTRACT	60p*
0426157206	THE KREMLIN FILE	60p*
0426140745	THE LIQUIDATOR	70p*
0426185501	THE LIST	60p*
0426126181	MACAO	70p*
0352304707	THE MARK OF COSA NOSTRA	60p*
0426180089	THE N3 CONSPIRACY	70p*
0426168704	OUR AGENT IN ROME IS MISSING	45p*
0352304677	RHODESIA	70p*
0426073177	THE SEA TRAP	70p*
0426180674	THE SIGN OF THE COBRA	60p*
0426184467	SIX BLOODY SUMMER DAYS	60p*
042612765X	THE SLAVEMASTER	70p*
0426185420	THE SNAKE FLAG CONSPIRACY	60p*
0426168895	THE SPANISH CONNECTION	45p*
0426185188	THE TURNCOAT	60p*
0426187377	THE ULTIMATE CODE	60p*
0426184114	THE Z DOCUMENT	60p*

†For sale in Britain and Ireland only
*Not for sale in Canada.
♦ Film & T.V tie-ins.

Wyndham Books are obtainable from many booksellers and newsagents. If you have any difficulty please send purchase price plus postage on the scale below to:

Wyndham Cash Sales:
P O Box 11,
Falmouth,
Cornwall.

or

Star Book Service:
G P O Box 29,
Douglas,
Isle of Man,
British Isles.

While every effort is made to keep prices low, it is sometimes necessary to increase prices at short notice. Wyndham Books reserve the right to show new retail prices on covers which may differ from those advertised in the text or elsewhere.

Postage and Packing Rate
UK
22p for the first book plus 10p per copy for each additional book ordered to a maximum charge of 82p.

BFPO and Eire
22p for the first book, plus 10p per copy for the next 6 books and thereafter 4p per book.

Overseas
30p for the first book and 10p per copy for each additional book.

These charges are subject to Post Office charge fluctuations.